Little Rooms

Little Rooms

JAMES LEWELLING

Published by
DEEP SETT PRESS

San Diego

First Published 2014

© James Lewelling 2014

Cover design by Ellen Harvey

Cover photograph by Joseph Hu.
Courtesy of the artist and Locks Gallery.

Library of Congress Control Number: 2013947763

ISBN 978-0-9890948-4-9

for Lisa

Henry: The perfect hotel room—rarely if ever available, but exactly what is required—must at all costs and regardless of the greatest inconveniences, hold itself pristinely above the twinned morasses of space and time, which are forever extruding up their tendrils towards it; as tendrils of lava might menace a line of laundry stretched along the shared rim of adjacent and disquieted craters. The perfect hotel room is not the room in which I am presently immersed with its spare collection of rented amenities. Nor is it the rat hole from which I've recently absconded, cluttered with the detritus of acquisition. Nor is it a mailbox of any kind, nor a happy home. The perfect hotel room is as neat and unlikely as a cat box lodged in a blasted tree after a tornado, the cat still pawing at the gravel. Or, conversely, it is as messy and commonplace as a bird cage snagged in an opened-basement corner after a flood, the bird still probing the seams with its beak.

Now, the room I find myself bottled in at this moment of congesting electric light is so far descended from that necessary ideal as to counterfeit the currency with which I acquired it, as I will demonstrate forthwith:

Let me bend back the mattress. Here. Just a minute. There. Back a little further in the lint. Under the bed's coaster. Ahh... yes, Exhibit A. Not much. A white corner folded. But let me unfold it for you. Yes. Here it is, a note from myself to myself, scrawled at the time I last occupied this inadequate space. That is in the past, mind you. Some days ago or months. It reads:

Dear Future Henry,

Be aware! The instance of temporal implosion you are now experiencing is itself only one new pinching shoe taken from a rack of shoes, each identical to that which you now hold, stiff and fragrant in your child's fingers, up to your face.

And so I, the you of the past, a different you but also the same you, offer up this single exhortation: Carry on good Henry and let not the past be your guide!

The magnate understands then that the project will never get finished...

Jack's grandfather wakes and sets out from his hut. The green-lozenged jungle wall shears open to receive him...

The girls pull on their stained tights. The cabby chokes his cab. Jack's father rolls over in his ditch...

Sherry pushes a cigarette out against the side of her shoe...

The doctor spits his stethoscope into his cupped hands and holds it there dripping...

Ralph nuzzles the purple belly of the sky...

The rats roll out of their holes...

Parson Smith opens his door from the inside...

Hello Jack! says Parson Smith. Hi! says Jack. You look great! I'm losing my hair, says Parson Smith. It's the hooch, says Jack. Maybe, says Parson Smith. But I believe it is occurring as a result of the conjugal relations I enjoy with my better half, Mary Smith. Could be, says Jack. How's the little guy? says Parson Smith. He's completely out of hand, says Jack. He's a monster. Talking now, is he? says Parson Smith. Yes, says Jack. He talks in complete sentences, and he refers to himself in the third person. Sit down on the couch beside Mary Smith, says Parson Smith, and we'll all have some hooch. Parson Smith motions to the couch with his long arm, which is meaty.

I could really use it, says Jack. That little guy is a real handful. He sure is. Then again, on some days he's not so bad. The days when he mostly sleeps, for example. On those days, when I've come back from a long evening of hooch drinking and conversation with you and your better half, Mary Smith, and I find him sleeping in the big orange chair, it's a real joy. It's a real joy for me to see him there sleeping.

But he's talking now, says Parson Smith. Yes, says Jack. These days when he has started talking in complete sentences and referring to himself in the third person are a completely different story. These

4

days his presence is much less like a joy and much more like a discomfiting and burdensome affliction that gives me the creeps. I'll get the hooch, says Parson Smith.

Mary Smith is sitting on the couch, watching the little people in the T.V. She is wearing a yellow house dress. The couch is red and lumpy. Jack shifts his weight around the lumps. Hello Mary Smith, says Jack. Hi Jack, says Mary Smith. I came from upstairs, says Jack. That was good of you, says Mary Smith. So good of you, Jack. You look great, Mary Smith, says Jack. Oh please, Jack, says Mary Smith. Look at the T.V. They're talking now, I'm sure, but I can't make out what it is they're saying. You look really great, says Jack. Here's the hooch, says Parson Smith, returning.

Here's to ya, says Jack. Here's to ya, says Mary Smith. Down she goes, says Parson Smith. That's fine hooch, says Jack. Sure is, says Parson Smith. Top shelf, says Jack. Always, says Parson Smith. I'll bet, says Mary Smith.

I mean that skeptically, says Mary Smith. The last time I went to the hooch depot there wasn't anything on the top shelf. The guy said, Look at this! And he swiped the top shelf with this finger, and the finger got all black. That indicated to me that the top shelf had been empty for some time. And then the guy said, I haven't seen the truck assigned to deliver the hooch that goes on the top shelf in a long while. That truck, if I remember correctly, was a white truck with a simple geometrical design on the side. The design was not white. The design was blue. It was blue.

That indicated to me, says Mary Smith, that there had been a crisis abroad and that crisis had interrupted either the production or distribution of the hooch designated to be displayed on the top shelf. I felt sad when I made that inference. I feel sad now remembering it. I feel as badly as I did the day I muddied my mother's laundry. I'll be right back, says Parson Smith.

On that day, says Mary Smith to Jack, I was a little girl. I played with the wind that then often visited our backyard. The backyard belonged to my mother, my father and I. Or so I thought. Actually the backyard belonged to a fourth party. I met this fourth party later in life. I was no longer a girl when I met him. I was a woman, and the appliances of women were available to me though I hardly knew then what use might have been made of them. I won't say I didn't try anyway, times being what they were. But this is all stuff and nonsense, isn't it Jack?

Well, says Jack.

The world was so clean when I was young, says Mary Smith. And then when I was not so young, it started getting dirty. Dirt got under my nails and in my hair and in my ears. I was thinking about laundry. My mother's laundry snapping in the wind in our backyard. I used to spend the long afternoons playing in the wind with the laundry snapping. This obsession. I can't get past it. One day, there I was on the shiny green grass with the white laundry snapping. My mother's face was in the window, smiling at me with all of her long mouth. I played and played and played. And then she went away. And then something happened. The thing that happened was so simple and formless. The wind shifted and disappeared. The sky folded into dusk. And the laundry was dirty. That's how simple it was. That's all it really took. Bring me something, Parson Smith! Sure thing, says Parson Smith, from the kitchen.

And from then on things began to be swallowed into normalcy, says Mary Smith to Jack. I met the fourth party who truly had possession of the backyard that I had formerly thought belonged to my mother, my father and I. And there was blood. But later that was swallowed into normalcy. And I met Parson Smith, and Parson Smith with his hooch and his absent hair is becoming swallowed into normalcy. And you, Jack? One day you will become swallowed into normalcy? says Mary Smith, becoming teary.

I sure wish Mona were here to enjoy this hooch with us, says Jack. When did you last see Mona? says Parson Smith, returning. It was in the fall sometime, I think, says Jack. I think it was in the morning, but I'm really not certain. Mary Smith starts to cry.

You see, says Jack. When Mona departed that fall morning, she said that she was only stepping out to pick something up, which she wished to consume upon her return that same morning. It was orange drink. She said, I'm stepping out now to purchase some orange drink, which I wish to consume upon my return this same morning. This orange drink, she said, will be cold, orange and sweet. And then she stepped out of the room, closed the door, and that was that.

I thought Mona would be returning imminently, so I took a nap. I dreamed in my nap about Mona's return. I dreamed she returned with a large jug of cold, sweet orange drink and we sat together on the sofa and drank it in front of the T.V. The little people in the T.V. were having a conversation while we were drinking though I couldn't make out exactly what they were saying.

I've had that dream, says Parson Smith. I had it shortly before I became a Parson.

That dream was a false dream, says Jack. It was false in that the events it depicted never came to pass. Or rather have yet to come to pass. It is possible that at some future date, the events depicted in that dream will come to pass, in which case and at which time, it will become a true dream. But, at the moment—that is now—it remains false.

I am growing melancholy, says Mary Smith, who has become convulsed with sobs. I'll get more hooch, says Parson Smith.

So you see, says Jack to Mary Smith. I hardly noticed the day Mona disappeared because on that day I was firmly convinced that she would reappear at any moment, and I remained firmly convinced for some time. So, now I cannot remember precisely which day she did disappear as that day is confused in my mind with the day I realized she had disappeared some time before and would not be returning imminently as I had been firmly convinced.

Oh Jack! says Mary Smith. My life with Parson Smith is a happy one and yet I am frequently plagued with regrets. It's the hooch, says Jack. No, says Mary Smith. I believe these moments occur as a result of the conjugal relations I enjoy with my better half, Parson Smith.

Jack looks Mary Smith right in her limpid eyes, which are precisely as dark and shiny as the black buttons sewn into the breast pocket of the Sunday suit which hangs in the back of Jack's smaller closet.

You might say, says Jack. That these moments of regret intrude themselves into even the most happy and well organized lives like clouds across the yellow sun. Oh Jack! says Mary Smith. And so too they pass like clouds, says Jack, leaving nothing in their wakes except the vague memory of their happenings. Oh Jack! says Mary Smith.

I'm back, says Parson Smith.

I just want to say, before we get any deeper into things, says Parson Smith, that you two, and I suppose Mona as well, were she here, which she isn't, but were she here, I wouldn't exclude her in spite of her well known short comings; short comings shared, I have reason to believe, by other members of the company; some closely related to myself; and such being the case, who am I? I ask you, who am I to cast stones? —are the very best and most esteemed of better halves and habitual acquaintances which I, in my long, seemingly interminable, sojourn in this nondescript and often disappointing vale have ever had the privilege of... privilege of...? Swilling hooch with in an atmosphere of congeniality and light, mutually confessional chat? says Jack. Exactly, says Parson Smith. Well put. Thank you, says Jack. Dry up, says Mary Smith, who has grown sour.

I am aware, says Mary Smith to Jack. That your occasional and occasionally sparkling eloquence is not unrehearsed. What? says Jack.

And that, in fact, were you not here, says Mary Smith, which you are of course, but were you not, you would probably be up in that high windswept room which you formerly shared with Mona, but that you now occupy with that horrid little guy. And were you there in that high windswept room with its oversized window rather than here in our squalid domicile, you would, in all likelihood, be standing in front of that oversized window of yours practicing your seemingly spontaneous eloquence; and if you were doing that instead of sitting here leering at me in the presence of my better half, Parson Smith, that repulsive little guy would be sitting on your shoulders practicing with you! Oh my, says Parson Smith. No, says Jack. Not in a million years.

I would never let the little guy get anywhere near my shoulders, says Jack. He really gives me the creeps, and besides that, I have good reason to believe he's dangerous. Why, just this morning I performed an experiment to find out just how dangerous he was.

The experiment was this: I got up, as usual, and after shaving and brushing my teeth and otherwise completing my morning toilet, as usual, I removed the little guy from the harness in the shower and dumped him wriggling and cursing into the orange chair, again as usual. But next, instead of leaving the building to wander the neighborhood in search of word of Mona among the ne'er-do-wells as I usually would have done, I only pretended to leave. I told the little guy to be good, as I always do, and left my room, closing the door behind me, as usual, but then instead of going out and about, I went out and circled behind. I padded down the front stairs, as usual, but then I circled around behind this very building and tip-toed up the fire escape stairs in back.

Those stairs, you might remember, are on the outside. That was the trick to it. You see the whole point of my little experiment, and I can call it mine because it was I who thought it up—last night, by myself, lying in bed, dreaming of Mona's return—was to see just exactly what the little guy would do were I not there to observe him doing it. But of course, I would be there, but not on the inside where he was, but on the outside, kneeling on the fire-escape with my chin propped on the cold concrete ledge of the small kitchen window, looking in. So what did he do? says Parson Smith.

He took out his shapes, says Jack. Shapes? says Parson Smith. He keeps them under the orange chair, says Jack. Sometimes he takes them out. Takes them out? says Mary Smith. Like this, says Jack.

Jack slides off the couch to sit Indian style on the orange carpet in front of Parson Smith and Mary Smith. He presses his fingers together so that his hands look like little snouts, raises the snouts to either side of his head and begins speaking:

I'm the big shape, says the big shape, says Jack in a low voice, wiggling the snout on the left side of his head. And I'm the little shape, says the little shape, says Jack in a high squeaky voice, wiggling the snout on the right side of his head.

They look like little dogs, says Mary Smith. They're not dogs, says Jack. They're shapes, but they talk like people. Listen!

Oh you are a nice little shape, says the big shape. I want to keep you here on the carpet with me. No, says the little shape. I am not nice and I prefer to remain under the orange chair. Shhh! Quiet! says the big shape Here comes Little Jack.

I'm Little Jack, says Little Jack.

And for me, says Jack, that's the creepiest part, the part where he refers to himself as 'Little Jack.' I think the whole thing is creepy, says Mary Smith. I don't get it, says Parson Smith. They're only shapes, says Jack. But they talk like people. Listen:

Oh Little Jack! says the big shape. We love you. Don't put us in the toaster where we will get singed. Oh Little Jack! says the little shape. You are the greatest! Don't put us in the sink where we will get soggy!

Or bunch us up in your fists, says the big shape. Or tear us with your fingers, says the little shape. Or put us in the freezer, says the big shape. Or chew us in your great mouth, says the little shape. Please! say both the shapes at the same time.

And then the little guy just got quiet, says Jack. And he looked at the shapes, moving first one and then the other closer and farther from his face, like this.

Jack brings first one and then the other bunched up hand close to his own face.

Then he said:

You are liars, says Little Jack, and the punishment for lying is death. Death by fire.

Then the little guy pulled the Mona matches out of his diaper, says Jack, and showed them to the shapes.

Those are really neato! says the little shape. Those are really cool! says the big shape. Shut up! says Little Jack. These Mona matches are the instruments of your destruction!

Mona matches? says Parson Smith.

I think the little guy stole them from the cupboard where I keep my hooch, says Jack. They're matches with a picture of Mona on them. In the picture Mona is sitting on her butt with her chin on her knees, and she's really white. The rest of the picture is black. It's my only and favorite picture of her. I see, says Parson Smith.

I don't think you do, says Jack. It's a really good picture of her. She forgot the matches when she left, and I keep them as a keepsake and to remind me what Mona used to look like should she be gone a considerable stretch of time. I see, says Mary Smith.

I don't think you do, says Jack. The little guy stole them from me. And just wait till you hear what he did with them. Listen:

Run away! says the big shape. Run away! says the little shape. If we scatter, he can't get all of us! say all the other shapes.

Then he stood up, says Jack, and all the shapes dropped out of his lap and he threw the two he was holding in his hands on the carpet and said:

The shapes try to scatter, but instead they are gathered up. They are gathered up in the hands of Little Jack.

You are silent now! says Little Jack. You are silent and you are waiting. You are waiting for the words of Little Jack.

Oh Little Jack! says the big shape. You are right to be angry with me and all the other shapes. We erred when we said that we loved you when our true feelings run much closer to intimidated indifference with a touch of loathing. We erred grievously, says the little shape. Grievously, say all the other shapes in the pile.

Yes, says Little Jack.

We have erred and we wish to make it up to you, says the big shape. In as much as we can, says the little shape. A small gesture, says the big shape, but it's the best that we can do. We hope it's enough, says the little shape, but we understand it might not be. Hope! say half the other shapes. Understand! say the other half.

And Little Jack is silent.

And he was silent, says Jack, for a long time.

I sat and watched him, and during his silence I began to notice how cold and hard the fire-escape was on my knees and how awkward my posture was in general. I really developed a craving for hooch, and thought about heading out to the hooch depot to try to cage swigs from passing ne'er-do-wells. But then

I thought I really shouldn't, as abandoning the experiment at that point would have been almost the same as not having performed it at all.

Finally, says Jack, the little guy wiggled the big shape again, but just a little as if to indicate timidity. He said:

And so if you must burn something, says the big shape, we offer you this little shape to burn rather than burning all of us with the terrible Mona matches.

What? says the little shape. Burn the little shape! say all the other shapes at the same time. Just one minute, says the little shape. Why not burn one of the nondescript shapes?

Shut up! say all the nondescript shapes.

Why not burn the big shape then? says the little shape.

Shut up! says the big shape.

Why not burn—

Shut up! says Little Jack. It is for little Jack to decide.

Then the little guy spread the pile of shapes out on the carpet so he could get a good look at each and every one. And then he picked out one of the nondescript shapes and said:

Not me! says the nondescript shape. Yes you, says Little Jack.

And sure enough, says Jack, the little guy picked up the Mona matches, lit one and burned the nondescript shape while he was holding it in his hand, and he made the most piteous and agonized screams for it as it burned. And when the flame reached his fingers, he dropped the shape on the carpet, still burning, and the scream it was making turned to moans and then whimpers and then a kind of choking rattle until the flame smoldered out completely.

Jack lets his hands drop into his lap, and looks up at Parson Smith and Mary Smith.

Wow! says Parson Smith. What did you do to him? says Mary Smith. Well, says Jack, I had abandoned my post and gone through the kitchen to where he was sitting by that time, and you can bet he was none too pleased to see me there towering over him. I was upset and a little disturbed. I'm a little disturbed now, says Mary Smith. I'll get more hooch, says Parson Smith.

I beat him, says Jack to Mary Smith, who has again become teary, but I didn't enjoy beating him. I know he is a sick creature more deserving of pity than wrath. I also know that while on the outside he appears to be horrid and inhuman, on the inside he is probably considerably less loathsome. Oh Jack! says Mary Smith, sobbing. You're so sensitive!

My father was a lot like the little guy, says Jack. And although I never had the opportunity—because he abandoned, or rather was driven out of the house by my stout and vigorous mother while I was still just a sprat of a lad and thoroughly outclassed weight-wise—I'm sure that if I had had the opportunity, it would have pained me to beat my father as much as it pained me to beat the little guy, who I am sure is also invested with a better nature which was undeserving of the beating but had to suffer through it as well.

You are as sensitive as my mother, says Mary Smith. Well, says Jack. She was universally regarded as an extremely sensitive woman, maybe too sensitive, says Mary Smith. My mother, says Jack, who was an absolute brute with the arms and tongue of a fishmonger, had known your mother way back when, and she often commented to me about your mother's sensitiveness, though not always in a positive light. My mother was a sensitive woman, says Mary Smith, and she was a liberal woman. I believe my mother also commented on that, says Jack.

She was a liberal woman, says Mary Smith. When I was a girl—with the exception of only a few behaviors I have since grown too delicate to mention—she allowed me to do whatever I wanted and go wherever I wished to go.

In fact, says Mary Smith, when I was a girl, I used to wander far and wide in the fields and copses beyond the confines of the small, green backyard that at the time I thought belonged to my mother, my father and I. I used to wander in the gray meadows and brownish fields around our residence, occasionally plunging into and finding shelter in the small copses of slender black trees with soggy orange leaves which grew in those fields at irregular intervals.

On the day I'm thinking of right now, says Mary Smith, the air was heavy and damp and the gray clouds were smeared against the sky. I feared rain, but I felt safe under my nice yellow wind breaker. I liked the sky that way then, and I believe I would like the sky that way today should it ever again take that form. But some things are always to be wanted but never to be had, aren't they Jack? says Mary Smith to Jack. Well, says Jack.

Whoa! Ho! says Parson Smith, returning. Look what I found on the back porch! Parson Smith deposits a bruised and squirming bundle in the lap of Mary Smith to which it clings with great force. Oh my! says Mary Smith.

It's the little guy! says Parson Smith. I went out to the back porch to get more hooch, and who should I find out there mucking around in the box where I keep my extra supply? The little guy about whom we have recently been speaking!

The little guy turns his face briefly away from Mary Smith's lap. Coo coo, says Little Jack, says the little guy to Jack.

Did you find any hooch? says Jack. No dice, says Parson Smith. I'll just skip right over to the hooch depot and get some more. Now keep an eye on my better half, Mary Smith, while I'm gone, says Parson Smith, winking at the little guy, who does not look up from Mary Smith's lap. I'll be back in a jiffy, my angel, says Parson Smith to Mary Smith.

Where were we? says Mary Smith to Jack. The sky? says Jack.

On that day with the sky precisely the way I like it, says Mary Smith. I plunged into one particular copse of thin black trees with orange leaves, took off my nice yellow wind breaker, spread it on the damp grass, lay my small body down on it and fell asleep.

Look! says Jack, the little guy has fallen asleep! And I think he fell asleep at exactly the same moment you said, "I fell asleep." Well, says Mary Smith. He's a real joy to me when he sleeps, says Jack, mostly because he's so quiet then. Look! His mouth is making small shapes but no sound is coming out! I can see that, says Mary Smith. You fell asleep? says Jack.

In a particular copse of thin black trees with soggy orange leaves on a rainy but not yet raining day, says Mary Smith, I fell asleep and in my sleeping, dreamed. The dream I had was thick and heavy and colored in purplish hues. I found myself sheltering among the rigging of a very large wooden ship, and the air was full of its creakings. There was a man on the ship, a large man, his name was Bob Smith.

Bob Smith? says Jack. Yes, says Mary Smith. That was my better half Parson Smith's name before he became a Parson. He was much different then. For example, he had hair. Of course, the Bob Smith in my dream bears no relation to either Parson Smith or the Bob Smith he was before he became a Parson. I was only a little girl when I was having this dream, and I hadn't yet met either one of them. I see, says Jack.

The Bob Smith in my dream, says Mary Smith, took my little hand in his much larger hand and led me across the gently swaying decks under all the purplish sails that were furling and unfurling in the dark wet wind which eddied around them.

Come to think of it, says Jack. I have also met a man by the name of Bob Smith, who also bore no relation to your better half, Parson Smith. In fact, when I met this Bob Smith, if I remember correctly, there was something strange about him. Something distinctive. The Bob Smith in my dream, says Mary Smith, was relatively indistinct, except for his exceptional size and his bald head, which was haloed in the torch light.

That's it, says Jack. He was marked. I met him outside the place near the big building in which conventions are sometimes held. I'd been hanging around there with the little guy, looking for something...

In my dream, says Mary Smith, I held tightly to the hand of the large Bob Smith as he led me across the gently swaying decks to a small cabin with a small round window which was yellow from the yellow light of a lamp glowing behind it. I wanted him to take me inside the small cabin with the yellow window but at the same time I felt a strong intimation that he wouldn't.

Oh look! says Jack. The little guy's burping in his sleep! There, there, says Mary Smith. It's all right when he burps, says Jack. It just means he ate something.

But that intimation was false, says Mary Smith. For the large Bob Smith did bring me into the small cabin with the yellow window, but before he did, he bent down so his big face was close to mine, pursed his lips and put a finger to them, indicating that no matter what I should see there, I should be quiet and that he was taking me into his special confidence.

That doesn't sound like the man I remember from outside the place near the big building in which conventions are sometimes held, says Jack. That man, who I believe was also called Bob Smith, was not the confiding type. He didn't even look like the confiding type. If I remember correctly, he said—

The man in my dream, Jack, says Mary Smith, was very confiding. He bent down so he could look into my small face and pursed the lips on his rather large face and brought one stout index finger to them to indicate that what he was about to reveal was a secret and that no matter what it should be I should remain quiet and that a confiding and confidential pact existed between us.

That may be, Mary Smith, says Jack, but the man I met in front of the place near the big building took an altogether different tack in his brief but significant dealings with me. In fact, He said—

And in we went, says Mary Smith, through a small wooden door which groaned on its rusted hinges as the large Bob Smith wrenched it open. And inside there was a small room with a large wooden table with a kerosene lamp and a large stack of papers on it. At the head of the table sat—

He said, says Jack. You're Jack, aren't you? You've come to this place near the big building to take care of some business, haven't you? And when he said that he looked down at the little guy.

What's that coming out of the little guy's mouth? says Mary Smith. I think he's spitting up, says Jack. That's disgusting, says Mary Smith. Give me a corner of your dress, says Jack.

At the head of the table, says Mary Smith, sat a certain party who, now that I think of it, bore an uncanny resemblance to the guy at the hooch depot. A bit like a twit? says Jack. Exactly, says Mary Smith.

The demeanor of this certain party made quite an impression on me, says Mary Smith. But what he said escapes me completely. Though I do remember he concluded his message abruptly and left. He concluded and left so abruptly, in fact, that both I and my special confidant, the large Bob Smith, stood there in that small swaying room beside the wooden table with its kerosene lamp and large stack of papers, wondering whether he had been there at all.

The man I remember as Bob Smith, says Jack, didn't introduce me to anyone at all, but he himself was abrupt. He just asked me those odd questions, which sounded more like accusations to me, then pointed to his bald head and said—

Yes, the close of that mysterious interview was abrupt, says Mary Smith. Bob Smith and I just stood there a moment wondering at it. Then the large Bob Smith led me down a staircase, which was really more like a ladder, under a small door in the floor of the cabin which he had revealed to me by removing an orange carpet.

He said, says Jack. I know your business. It's as clear as day. But you—and he pointed at me—and that—and he pointed at the little guy—don't have a clue—

There is something very wrong with this child, says Mary Smith. I think the corner of my dress may be impeding his respiration. Maybe we should take him to that nursery I erected with my own hands way back when you and your better half, Parson Smith, were expecting a blessed gift from above? says Jack.

Oh that, says Mary Smith.

I was pleased to do it even though I am, and was then, only a casual acquaintance of yours, says Jack. And I remained pleased that I'd done it even after it became apparent that that blessed gift had been forestalled indefinitely.

Oh Jack, says Mary Smith.

C'mon, says Jack. Perhaps the little guy can test the nursery out. Then when your blessed gift comes, you can be sure all the bugs have been worked out of it. I don't know, says Mary Smith.

C'mon, says Jack, rising. Mary Smith rises as well, cradling the little guy, who has swallowed a considerable portion of the skirt of her dress, against her belly. They pass through a small door in the wall and up a short staircase to the nursery.

You did a wonderful job, says Mary Smith. It's so blue and comfortable and airy and the sky you painted is... But what's that thing curving around the eye of the moon? I have accentuated the moon's already lush and extravagant eyelash, says Jack, with a swathe of mascara. It's intended to emphasize its femininity. Hmm, says Mary Smith. C'mon little guy, says Jack prying the little guy from Mary Smith's belly and dumping him into the cradle. He doesn't seem to want to let go of my dress, says Mary Smith. He'll spit it out in a minute, says Jack.

The hold of that great and rolling ship struck me with a sense of comfort and airiness not unlike what you have ingeniously created in this small and windowless room, says Mary Smith. Hold? says Jack. That was where the ladder under the small door hidden beneath the orange carpet pulled away by the large Bob Smith led, says Mary Smith. Right, says Jack.

Bob Smith disappeared into that hold carrying with him the kerosene lamp, says Mary Smith, and when he did so the light moved in a strange and beautiful way; not unlike the way in which a bubble of air might move from one frozen under water chamber to another at the onset of an untimely thaw. I see, says Jack.

I don't think you do, says Mary Smith. You see I followed Bob Smith and saw the light from the lantern become a bubble of light, and that bubble of light was sucked as a bubble of air might be, out of that small room, plunging it into darkness. Darkness, says Jack. Only to expand again in the large and airy hold beneath it, says Mary Smith.

Do you think we ought to call a doctor or a specialist of some sort? says Mary Smith, pulling on the skirt of her dress with both hands. I don't believe I will be able to extricate the corner of my dress from the little guy's mouth without some assistance.

There was a doctor, says Jack, or at least a man who dressed like a doctor at that place near the big building where I met the terse and abrupt man I remember as Bob Smith.

There must be some trick to this, says Mary Smith.

That doctor, if he was a doctor, says Jack, was no help at all. He tried to hurry past the little guy and me but I stopped him with an inquiring look.

Are you sure, Jack, says Mary Smith, that you don't know any trick or stratagem that might be employed in this dilemma? The way he is convulsing is making me nervous.

He was harassed by the look I gave him, says Jack. He stopped and spoke dismissively to me and the little guy. He said, the facility is closed today. Take that home with you now, and if you wish, return at a more opportune time. And he left, and the tail of his lab coat fluttered behind him as he did so. Fluttered? says Mary Smith, collapsing beside the cradle with the skirt of her dress hiked nearly over her shoulders.

What do you think of that? says Jack.

The hold of the ship was filled with light bulbs, says Mary Smith. Frosted white light bulbs. They weren't stacked or boxed or sorted. They filled the bottom of the ship like an immense pile of loose eggs.

I think that man was acting rudely and unprofessionally, says Jack.

Mary Smith starts to cry. Jack reaches into the cradle and pinches the blue nose between the little guy's white eyes, the pupils of which have rolled up into his head. There you go, little guy, says Jack. Have you done it? says Mary Smith, rising. The little guy begins to shriek. The guy with the hooch is back! booms the voice of Parson Smith from below. The little guy shuts up. Good as new, says Jack. Stay here and be quiet! says Mary Smith, and she bustles down the stairs...

She's quite a number ain't she? says Jack to the little guy. And wandering! And liberal! Too bad I didn't get to bring this out. Jack reaches into his shirt and pulls out a small, black heart-shaped bottle with an indecipherable label. It's been known to work, little guy, says Jack. It's been known to work wonders. Jack sucks, says Little Jack, says the little guy.

(Where is that no good hooch swilling bastard? booms Parson Smith from below. And what's all that crap on your dress? If you are referring to our good neighbor, Jack, says Mary Smith, you were gone so long that he decided to retire to his high wind swept room and he quite responsibly took the child with him.)

Now what do we do? says Jack. Jack sucks big time, says Little Jack, says the little guy, standing up in the cradle beneath the extravagant lash of the moon.

(Yes, I have been to the hooch depot, booms Parson Smith. And yes, I have bought an exceptionally large bottle of hooch! But don't thank me for it, you hussy, because in addition to accomplishing my set purpose, I have also, quite by chance, heard certain things both at the hooch depot and on my way back from the hooch depot. Certain things closely concerning yourself. Oh dear, hush, says Mary Smith.

As you know, says Parson Smith, not too long ago I stepped out that door and into the dark and furtive night in quest of some hooch for my dearly beloved better half and our mutual acquaintance, Jack; both of whom, I might add, I had eulogized tearfully and sincerely, if a bit drunkenly, earlier in the evening. Come, come, says Mary Smith.

And the night was dark, furtive and crowded with furry presences scurrying here and there, says Parson Smith. But what was that to me? I was out on an errand on behalf of my better half and a long-standing acquaintance of ours. Why should I bother about unsanitary conditions in the world at large? Oh please, says Mary Smith.

I could see the hooch depot on the corner with its large picture window glowing yellow, says Parson Smith, and I walked resolutely towards it, amusing myself as I walked by watching the graceful oscillations of my shadow which kept swinging out in front of me and snapping back behind as I glided beneath the pale and luminous skirts of intermittent street lights. Huh? says Mary Smith.

I amused myself that way, says Parson Smith. And I may even have whistled. Yes, I believe I whistled also as I went. You've always been such a good whistler, says Mary Smith.)

They're lying there, says Jack to the little guy. Parson Smith and I once had a whistling contest at a certain convention just to pass the time, and if I remember correctly, Parson Smith was completely incapable. He'd purse his lips together and blow, but nothing ever came out but little bits of spit and air. He was a real king loser when it came to whistling.

(I whistled, says Parson Smith. I did, just to amuse myself, and soon enough I had reached the hooch depot and pushed open the glass door, and a bell rang signaling my arrival. And who do you think was in that box of light perched on the corner?

I'll tell you who, your old pal, the guy at the hooch depot, that's who. And there was another guy there too. He had a cabby's hat on and an enormous nose. Was he your old pal too? The guy with the enormous nose? Oh please, Parson Smith, Mary Smith says. I don't know what you're talking about.

I ignored the cabby, says Parson Smith, and walked straight up to the guy, who was sitting behind the counter reading a paper, and said, My wife sent me out for more hooch.

That's exactly what I said even though you hadn't sent me out but I'd come on my own initiative. I said, "My wife" by which I meant you, my own better half "sent me" by which I meant me, your own better half, Parson Smith "out for some hooch" by which I meant this exceptionally large bottle from which I have been pouring tumblers since I began this harangue! I said it that way to indicate to the guy at the hooch depot and indeed the world at large, that I, Parson Smith had such respect, nay reverence, for you, Mary Smith, that I was not ashamed to be sent out on trivial errands by you but would cheerfully carry them out with dispatch and I didn't care a whit who knew about it!

But the guy didn't even look up from his newspaper, says Parson Smith. So I waited a moment, and explained it to him again. I said, A long-standing acquaintance of ours came over this evening and swilled hooch with us. So now we're out, and my wife sent me here for some more. And without lowering the paper, the guy asked me right off the bat, What's your wife's name? And I said, Mary Smith, and he said, Oh yeah, I know that one.

I know that one, he said! says Parson Smith. Just like that. But fool that I was, I didn't make anything of it. I just went on to explain about our names. My name is Parson Smith, I said, but it's just a coincidence. Mary Smith was Mary Smith before she met me, and when we were married she chose not to adopt my name. Similarly, I was Parson Smith before I met her, and when we were married, I also chose not to adopt her name.

But the guy wasn't listening. He was still reading his paper. But then he stopped and spread the paper on the counter and turned it around toward me and said, Will you look at this? I think the Commandant has made another announcement, but I can't quite make out what it is. The Commandant? I said. He's a maniac, I think, said the guy. His country makes a lot of hooch. I looked at the paper but it didn't make any sense to me either. It's not good news though, said the guy. In fact, I'm pretty sure it's bad news, but I haven't a clue what kind of bad news it is. Even when I understand one of his announcements word for word, the import often escapes me completely. For that, you have to wait for its effects. After you've seen the effects, the message becomes all too clear and it's hard to believe you hadn't understood it in the first place.

See, said the guy, adopting a tone I found rather over-confiding. I have this the theory that an announcement that appears neutral or even benign on its face—that is, in the words—will more often than not prove to have been negative or extremely negative once you've seen its effects. For example, one of the chief effects of just about any announcement seems to be an interruption in the flow of hooch to this retail outlet, and when there is a prolonged interruption, our inventory drops to zero and when that happens, things can get pretty crazy. Crazy? I said, not having the slightest idea of what he was talking about.

Really crazy, said the guy. That's why I keep this gun here with me.

And right then and there, without the least provocation from me, he pulled a shiny double barreled shot gun from under the counter, and pointed it at me and said, Have you ever been seized with an irresistible compulsion?

I didn't have the faintest clue as to what he was talking about, says Parson Smith. I just wanted some hooch. But maybe you would have known, my better half, Mary Smith. Maybe irresistible compulsions are right up your alley. Oh ple— says Mary Smith.

Of course not, said the guy, without lowering the gun, says Parson Smith. I can tell just by looking at you. People who have been seized with irresistible compulsions can usually recognize people who haven't. Customers who have become accustomed to a regular and uninterrupted supply of hooch often become seized with irresistible compulsions when their supply is interrupted. These compulsions usually assume a destructive aspect, destructive toward people or property or both.

For example, said the guy, you've ventured out in the dark and furry night this evening in quest of hooch, haven't you? Well, I said. And to that end, you have penetrated this well lit box in which hooch is habitually dispensed, haven't you? said the guy. Well, I said. And in coming here, you have developed a hearty expectation that your request will be vouchsafed, haven't you? said the guy. Well, I said.

Now, just suppose, he said, that there wasn't any hooch available here. You'd naturally become disappointed and disgruntled. Maybe extremely disappointed and disgruntled, he said. And in your extreme disgruntlement, you might become seized with an irresistible compulsion which, in all likelihood, would take on a destructive aspect toward my person or property or both.

I didn't have anything to say, says Parson Smith.

That's why I have this shotgun here, he said, patting the barrel of the gun. Not, as you might at first think, to deter you from carrying out the inspiration of your disgruntlement, but to dispatch you forthwith, as I know from first hand experience that deterrence in the face of irresistible compulsions is completely superfluous.

My better half, Mary Smith, I said, sent me out for more hooch.

Maaarreee Smith! he said, and put the shotgun down on the counter. Bingo! I said.

Earlier, he said, when I indicated to you that I knew your better half, Mary Smith, by saying "Oh I know that one" I was speaking in a bored, desultory fashion without, in fact, recalling the person in question. I always say that when someone speaks in my presence of a third party who is not present. I do that to give the impression of omniscience. Omniscience? I said. But in the present instance, he said, I do recall the person you referred to. Mary Smith, I said.

Maaarree Smith! he said again, and the way he said it meant a lot. Comes in here all the time, he said. Quite a number, ain't she?

Quite a number! Quite a number, he called you!! says Parson Smith. Now what exactly does *that* mean? I'm sure I don't know, says Mary Smith.

And then the cabby, who had been standing there the whole time with his big nose pressed flat against the window, felt obliged to turn towards us and chime in, Maaarree Smith! Boy oh boy!

Now what did *that* mean? says Parson Smith. I'm afraid I can't tell you, says Mary Smith, as I don't believe I have ever encountered either of the gentlemen in question on anything other than trivial occasions.

Well, says Parson Smith. You can bet I didn't choose to investigate the matter right then and there. Why should I denude my shame any more than it had already been denuded?

Excuse me? I said, in highly dignified tones. And you're her better half, Parson Smith, said the guy. She speaks very highly of you. Now what kind of hooch do you want? One large bottle please, I said, all business. Y'know, he said, there are more efficacious, indeed permanent, ways to chase the blues than hooch drinking. I don't drink hooch to chase the blues, I informed him. For me, the consumption of hooch merely provides the focus of social interaction among myself, my better half, Mary Smith, our acquaintance, Jack, and his girlfriend, Mona. Mona? the guy said.)

Mona? says Jack. Mona? says Little Jack, says the little guy.

(We have, I said, often gathered around a bottle of your finest hooch to recount our various and disparate experiences and in that way warm our inexorably cooling souls in the tepid and often moist glow of communion thus produced.

I was trying to elevate him, says Parson Smith, but he wasn't really listening. All he said was, Mona.)

Mona! says Jack. Coo coo! Mona Mona! says Little Jack, says the little guy.

(I have never consumed hooch outside of that context, I said, but my better half, Mary Smith, is a completely different story. She'll drink hooch morning, noon and night with or without company. It's all the same to her. She's a lush.

I thought he should know about your proclivities should you ever attempt to formalize whatever sordid rapport exists between you, says Parson Smith. You're a real suck, says Mary Smith, who has once again grown sour.

But he seemed to already know all about it because he pulled a business card out of his pocket, and pushed it across the counter toward me. Send her to this address, he said. There's a guy there who will take care of it. He'll take care of it once and for all. Thanks for the tip, I said, and I took that card and I put it in my pocket and it's in my pocket right now. Who knows? We might need it some day. Are you finished now? says Mary Smith. No, says Parson Smith. The worst part is coming up. Oh please, says Mary Smith.

You know that for some time now, says Parson Smith, I have been experiencing moments of miraculous and extrasensory communication with the beasts of the field. Well, says Mary Smith. Birds, for example, or that incident with the squirrel, says Parson Smith. Well, says Mary Smith. I remember you telling me about it, but quite frankly I assumed you were talking about something completely different. I wasn't, says Parson Smith. I was speaking literally and without guile, just as I am right now.

It happened again, says Parson Smith, as I was dragging this exceptionally large bottle of hooch along the sidewalk home. Just as I reached our front walk, I noticed a small furtive movement near the corner of this very building. As I looked closer I realized that that movement was being performed by a vile rodent of the sewer rat variety. That's disgusting, says Mary Smith.)

Rats?! says Little Jack, says the little guy.

(Yes, it was, says Parson Smith. As I approached the building and drew closer to the rat, I could see that it was yellow of tooth, its back was a stunted tangle and its yellow eyes gleamed white with fever. Just after I managed to pull the door open and was wrestling this exceptionally large bottle of hooch into the vestibule, the rat looked up at me from the corner of the building, and the two of us communicated in a mysterious fashion.

Ho! Vile night traveler! What unsavory business brings you here at this hour? I said though "said" is not the right word for it.

Dry up! Why should I tell you? said the rat. Is rat business, your business? Certainly not, I said, but I live in this residence and thus have an interest in your dealings here. Ask your better half, Mary Smith, said the rat and then it hopped around the corner in the most loathsome fashion imaginable.)

The rats are coming for Little Jack! says Little Jack, says the little guy. Shhh! says Jack.

(Well, says Parson Smith. The guy at the hooch depot and the deformed cabby weren't enough for you? You've descended into the lower orders to quench your unwholesome lusts? You've very plainly lost your mind, says Mary Smith. Pour me more hooch and let's talk about something else.

Maybe I have lost my mind, says Parson Smith. Maybe I lost it long before I met you. But I remain concerned about your habits and there's something I need to show you.

There is the sound of the couch groaning, and then the noise of a closet door being slid open on its tracks.

It's something my father gave me, says the muffled voice of Parson Smith. I've been meaning to show you his gift to me for a long time but I've always been distracted at the last moment. Oh God! Your father! says Mary Smith.

He was an upright character, says the muffled voice of Parson Smith, and steadfast. I never liked your father, says Mary Smith. But he liked you, says the muffled voice of Parson Smith. From the first time he met you. I remember shortly after that occasion, he interrupted a bath I was then taking to tell me so. I met your father long before I met you, murmurs Mary Smith, wringing one finger in her lap.

He came into the bathroom unannounced as was his habit, says Parson Smith, his voice getting louder as he steps out of the closet, dragging something heavy and jangly across the carpet.

He was wearing blue slacks, says Parson Smith. He sat himself on the edge of the tub and said, That little girl Mary Smith you just met, she's quite a number, ain't she?

You should dry up, Parson Smith, says Mary Smith. You should dry up and blow away, "leaving only a vague memory in your wake like a" like a... A cloud across the yellow sun? says Parson Smith. Oh Jack! says Mary Smith.

You were right before, says Parson Smith, when you suggested that his eloquence is not unrehearsed. It's my suspicion that that eloquence is not only not unrehearsed, but not original either. It's my suspicion that the little guy makes it all up before hand, and tells Jack exactly what to say.)

Little Jack is Little Jack! says the little guy, rising in the cradle. Shut up, says Jack.

(Leave the little guy out of it, says Mary Smith. It's also my suspicion, says Parson Smith. That behind that fake eloquence and perpetually sunny but thoughtful disposition lurks the spotted soul of a ne'er-do-well just as was the case with his father before him. I am not unaware that he pleases you.

What? says Mary Smith.

And that the manner in which you react to him is not completely without amorous overtones, says Parson Smith. Really, says Mary Smith.

There is the sound of a cardboard box being slit open with a razor or some other very sharp implement. The tape on the box screams tightly as it is split.

I have not the smallest of amorous inclinations towards Jack, says Mary Smith. Honest!

That may be my angel, says Parson Smith, whose voice has grown muffled once again, as if he has plunged his whole head and torso into the cardboard box.

That is, I believe you are utterly sincere when you say that. But—

He's really so average, says Mary Smith. So terribly, terribly average.

Can anyone know his own deepest inclinations? says the voice of Parson Smith from somewhere deep inside the box. At its most profound, is not the human soul relentlessly chimera and forever inscrutable to even the most vigilant of its proprietors?

Parson Smith grunts and drops something heavy on the floor. I'm not going to get into that thing, says Mary Smith.

I understand completely, my darling, says Parson Smith. I too was intimidated and reluctant the first time my father brought out this apparatus and strongly suggested, even insisted, that I employ it for my own self improvement. Your father was a sick fuck, says Mary Smith. He wore black ladies' support hose under his trousers, and when he adopted certain postures they made him look completely ridiculous! But just as I did, you misconceive the apparatus, says Parson Smith. One doesn't get into the apparatus. That's not it at all. The apparatus is not a coop or coral or cage of any kind. On the contrary, it is an article of adornment. One does not get into the apparatus. It's much more a matter of putting it on.

I don't know, says Mary Smith.

The apparatus, says Parson Smith, restrains without restricting. It covers without obscuring. It molds without distorting the tender material entrusted to its tender grasp.

I don't know, says Mary Smith.

And best of all, says Parson Smith, everything is reciprocated. As it restrains, so too is it restrained. As it covers, so too is it covered. As it molds, so too is it given shape. Of course it takes some getting used to. But as you get used to it, so too will it get used to you!

Oh I remember, says Parson Smith, I too protested bitterly before finally acceding to my father's loving request, and indeed I remember protesting for some time after I had done so. But soon enough—actually it took some time, I have difficulty remembering how much time, in fact, it might have been a long time, or an interminably long time—I came to understand the apparatus's native genius, and now I am sure I am a better man, though not without my failings, for having come to understand it, and if my father were here today I would kiss his folded hands with gratitude.

I don't know, says Mary Smith.

Let me help you, says Parson Smith, and there is the sound of shuffling, snapping canvas and metal buckles jangling.   Mary Smith starts to say something but her voice is instantly swallowed up.

There, says Parson Smith, grunting. Move your foot a little. Ahh yes... The nose... Over here. Can you feel your shoulder? Just a sec. To the right. It would help if you made a shimmying motion now. Ahh... Parson Smith sighs deeply, and all is quiet for some time.)

I wonder what he did to Mary Smith, says Jack. Jack is a moron, says Little Jack, says the little guy.

The silence continues for a long time, interrupted only by intermittent thumps reminiscent of the thumps a very large fish might make as it twists and writhes in the bottom of a boat. After a while, these thumps desist. Parson Smith's voice can be heard again.

(Are you O.K. in there? says Parson Smith. No, you're not O.K.

There is the sound of a thick, cloth belt whirring through a buckle.

None of us is O.K., says Parson Smith.

There is the sound of a strap being cinched tight.

We have not been O.K. since the arrival of the little guy in the room of Jack and Mona, and we were not O. K. before his arrival, says Parson Smith.

One and then another snap is fastened with a bright click.

My father, though an upright character of unquestionable integrity, was not O.K., says Parson Smith, and there is the sound of canvas being dragged across the carpet.

Jack's ne'er-do-well father and exotic grandfather were not O.K. by any stretch of the imagination. Uhhgg...

Parson Smith grunts and the couch groans.

Sometimes Mary Smith, says Parson Smith, I become poignantly aware of my own not-O.K.-ness. In those moments, that not-O.K.-ness becomes a Parson Smith-shaped thing identical to, and yet apart from, myself...

Everything is quiet for a long time.)

The little guy falls asleep in the cradle. Jack sits on the floor, waiting. He waits for a long time, and then he waits some more. I'm just waiting here, Jack thinks, and there is not another thought in his head. Then the sound of deep, mellow sonorous snores reaches him from below. C'mon little guy, Jack says.

The lights are out in the living room. The dark bulky form of Parson Smith can be seen on the floor slumped against the sofa. A similarly large and bulky form can be seen stretched out on the sofa. This form is covered with canvas, shaped roughly like a huge garment bag and covered with straps and buckles which glint in the pale smears of light leaking in through the front window.

Hee, hee, hee, says Jack, setting the little guy on the floor. Jack tip-toes around the form on the couch, loosening straps and undoing buckles. When he finishes, he pulls out the black, heart-shaped bottle from his shirt and places it on the floor next to the sofa. Hee, hee, hee, says Jack, scooping up the little guy...

* * * * *

Here he comes, says the first child on the landing to a second perched further up the stairs. Go get him and bring him up here, says the second child, disappearing up around a corner.

Hey mister! says the first child to Jack, who stands blinking in the brightly lit hall, with the little guy cradled in his arms. Why don't you come upstairs with me and have a chat? Huh? says Jack. Why don't you come upstairs with me and have a chat?

says the first child. Oh... you, says Jack. Why don't you leave me alone? And don't think I don't know your buddy is hanging around here somewhere. There is a giggling from above. Yeah, says Jack, there he is.

We've seen you a lot in your comings and goings, says the first child. And we want to know why in all those comings and goings you haven't ever come up and visited us. Shut up! says Jack. Comings and goings, it's always the same, and what business is it of mine? I have just spent a rather long and congenial evening in the company of my acquaintances, Parson Smith and Mary Smith, and am now returning to my own domicile to sleep it off as they say. Why would I want to have anything to do with the likes of you?

We might have something for you, says the first child. Something you'd really like, says the voice of the second child, wafting down the stairs. I'll bet, says Jack.

I mean that skeptically, says Jack. My father—who, though a ne'er-do-well, was not without his good qualities way back when—once succumbed to a similar invitation from parties not unlike yourselves and it didn't go well for him. It didn't go well at all.

He's talking about his father, the child calls up the stairs. Oh gee! says the second child.

In fact, says Jack, if I remember correctly, previous to succumbing to that invitation from those parties not unlike yourselves, my father—though already well along in the course of his degeneration and already branded a ne'er-do-well by my stout and vigorous mother as well as the community at large— had still exhibited certain gentler and more elevated qualities on rare but persistent occasions. Huh? says the first child. A rogue's generosity was occasionally displayed, for example, says Jack. I also often detected a softness in his manner toward certain birds and children. That's us! says the voice of the second child.

You might say, says Jack, that these signs I mention, as fleeting as they were, may have indicated the existence of a kind of inner visage—one of gentle line and soft complexion—existing beneath the face he displayed to the world, which was itself uncompromisingly degenerate.

And so, if you'll excuse me, says Jack, pushing past the first child to stumble up the steps where he comes face to face with the second child, whose face, it might be added, is identical to the face of the first—that is perhaps unusually pale but otherwise completely generic.

The present isn't for you, says the second child. It's for Little Jack.

The rats are coming for Little Jack! says Little Jack, says the little guy. Shut up! Jack says to the little guy.

There is no such person, Jack says to the second child. And if you are referring to this little guy who I am carrying clutched to my breast, I assure you he has everything he needs.

The rats are coming for Little Jack!! insists Little Jack, says the little guy. Shut up! says Jack, and pushing past the second child, he opens the door to his own room, enters and shuts the door firmly behind him.

Why don't you shut up and sleep here in the orange chair, says Jack, dumping the little guy into the orange chair. THE RATS ARE COMING FOR LITTLE JACK!!! SAYS LITTLE JACK, says the little guy.

I really wish you wouldn't call yourself that, says Jack. When you call yourself that, it gives me the creeps. It gives me the creeps first off because you are referring to yourself in the third person like a madman or an idiot, and second off because you are not Little Jack! Little Jack is Little Jack, says Little Jack, says the little guy.

Jack gets down on his knees in front of the orange chair and puts his face really close to the face of the little guy.

You're not Little Jack, says Jack, whose eyes are bloodshot and whose mouth is slack, dripping and smells of hooch. You're just a little guy who somehow got into our room. And then what were we to do, Mona and I? We didn't have options. I remember that day clearly. It was in the spring. The world seemed especially fresh, wet and waiting. Mona got restless. We decided to give the room the once over. We moved the couch, and there you were wrapped up like a sausage beneath it. No telling how long you'd been there. Mona said, Let's take him to that place over by the big building. But I said, We can't take him to that place. He's just a little guy. We can't keep him here, said Mona. But I said, We can keep him here. We can keep him here for a while. Little Jack is Little Jack, says the little guy.

Oh boy, says Jack, rising. Jack lumbers off to the kitchen. His voice gets smaller as he moves away.

You didn't give Mona the creeps, says Jack. She said, Let's take him to that place by the big building. That's what she said. She's unflappable. Or at least she was when she was here. I don't know if she remains unflappable out there among the ne'er-do-wells. It's possible they really get to her though she would never say so. She might say, those ne'er-do-wells really get to me sometimes. But she would say it in a manner that indicated that she didn't really mean it. But maybe even speaking in that manner to a casual interlocutor, she would at the same time be speaking to herself in an altogether different manner; one in which her statements were not ironic. That's not unheard of. I often wonder about that, little guy. You remember Mona, don't you? Jack calls from the kitchen.

Of course you do, Jack says returning, his voice getting larger as he comes closer.

You were as crazy about her as I was, says Jack. Maybe more. Some people might even say your affections for Mona were untoward. Parson Smith and Mary Smith, for example, might consider your affections untoward, but only Mary Smith would say it. In fact, she did say it to me just before they departed the last time they were over. They had both observed you locked around Mona's leg all evening as we drank hooch and Mona recounted her earlier more congenial days hanging around the hooch depot in that other town she comes from. But Parson Smith only said, Whoa there little guy! as I might have said. But Mary Smith, as they were leaving, paused just past the threshold of this very room and leaned her head back into the doorway, and whispered, His affections for Mona are a tad untoward, aren't they, Jack?

Jack's face is very big in front of the face of the little guy. His teeth are especially big and his nose.

You suck! says Little Jack, says the little guy. We're gonna play a game now, says Jack and the whites of his eyes turn yellow. You're a freak! says Little Jack, says the little guy. C'mon little guy, says Jack, scooping up the little guy once again. We're gonna play "Let's Teach the Little Guy How to Swim." The little guy starts to scream but Jack claps his big, smelly hand over his mouth.

It's not that I blame you for Mona's disappearance, says Jack, lumbering toward the bathroom. Like I said, Mona was unflappable. You didn't give her the creeps. She didn't leave that morning because of you. Not strictly because of you. I wouldn't say you drove her out. No, not exactly that. You could have been more congenial though. Your affections were a tad untoward. Mona did say at one point, it's getting so I can hardly walk around with this little guy clamped to my leg.

Jack pushes open the bathroom door and makes a very loud sound. He makes the sound because the little guy has bitten his hand and broken through the skin. Whoa there little guy! says Jack, turning on the tub faucet. Little Jack would prefer not to play, says Little Jack, says the little guy.

There is a knock on Jack's door.

Jack? says a voice from the hallway. I think you've forgotten something, Jack.

Jack pauses a moment, bent over the tub with the little guy under his arm. Then he drops the little guy into the tub. Hee hee hee, says Jack, tiptoeing over to the front door.

Just a minute, says Jack.

Oh Jack, says the voice. Thank goodness you're awake. I thought, perhaps, you would be sleeping. I thought, perhaps, you would be unconscious or otherwise unavailable to me when I came up here.

Yes? says Jack.

He fell asleep some time ago, says the voice. Even now his form slumps heavily on our nuptial mattress like a huge sack of grain. But not completely like a sack of grain because it is sweating, says the voice.

Sweating? says Jack.

And breathing, says the voice. Oh Jack! It's too horrible. Jack, Jack, Jack, Jack!

Hee hee hee, says Jack under his breath, and then more loudly. What do you want? Are you from the hooch depot?

I brought you something, says the voice, I brought you something you forgot downstairs.

Jack opens his door from the inside. Mary Smith is standing in the hall, clad in a white nighty and holding a black plastic shopping bag against her chest.

Mary Smith! says Jack. Jack! says Mary Smith. Come in! says Jack. Thank you! says Mary Smith. I've been giving the little guy a bath, says Jack. Make yourself at home. Would you like some hooch? Jack says, disappearing into the kitchen. I could sure use it, says Mary Smith. There's not much left, says Jack, from the kitchen. But what I've got is yours.

Oh dear, says Mary Smith, looking down at the little guy who has slipped out of the bathroom and clamped his arms and legs around one of her thighs. The rats are coming for Little Jack, says Little Jack, says the little guy, quietly.

I had an ample supply at one time, says Jack. I kept it in a large box under the sink.

Jack? says Mary Smith.

But Mona took it, says Jack, returning, when she left. For a long time I thought I had simply misplaced it, but then I realized Mona wasn't going to come back imminently as I had supposed, and I put two and two together, if you know what I mean. I understand perfectly, says Mary Smith, and thank you very much for admitting me at such a late hour. I don't suppose you could separate the little guy from my leg to which he seems to have attached himself?

He must like you, says Jack. He's normally distrustful of strangers. But not in my case, says Mary Smith. No, says Jack, delicately sipping at his hooch. Not with you. There must be something about you. Thank you, says Mary Smith. I often hear that. Because it's true, says Jack. You shouldn't dismiss such comments or let them pass completely unacknowledged, but allow yourself to indulge just a bit in the fleeting pleasure of each as you would in a finger touch of admiration. Oh Jack! says Mary Smith. It's true, says Jack. What have you brought me?

Well, says Mary Smith. I hardly know where to start. I'd like to put this delicately if I can. Is it a present? says Jack. No, says Mary Smith. Not exactly. Actually I'm glad it's not a present, says Jack. Presents, I have heard, often carry with them a tacit but very real bond of mutual obligation. I wouldn't want anything like that to insinuate itself into my relations with you and your better half, Parson Smith. Oh no, says Mary Smith.

Those relations, as far as I have been concerned, have been completely satisfactory, as I hope they have been for you and your better half, Parson Smith, says Jack. Of course, says Mary Smith. And the most satisfying aspect of them, says Jack, has been their crystalline and ingenuous nature. As saran wrap does not conceal the leftovers around which it clings, says Mary Smith, neither has our superficial discourse together concealed its import. Well put, says Jack. Thank you, says Mary Smith. How is your better half Parson Smith? says Jack.

He's sleeping, says Mary Smith. I confess the sight of his hulking form prostrate on the mattress, sweating and breathing, occasionally fills me with revulsion. That is unfortunate, says Jack. Yes, says Mary Smith. The revulsion I feel is sometimes so intense that I am unable to sleep. I see, says Jack. As is the case now, says Mary Smith. I see, says Jack. I had been sleeping, says Mary Smith, and, in fact, dreaming in my sleep but the feelings of revulsion I had for the hulking form of Parson Smith woke me from my dream. So I got up and wandered about the still emptiness of our domicile in my white nighty, like this.

Mary Smith rises and attempts to glide about the apartment, hampered somewhat by the black plastic shopping bag clutched to her chest and the little guy clamped to her leg.

You look just like a ghost, says Jack.

And in my wanderings, says Mary Smith. I found this! She thrusts the black shopping bag out for Jack to inspect.

I see, says Jack.

No, you don't, says Mary Smith. For inside this black shopping bag there is an item which I believe you must have left in our apartment because I don't recall stumbling across it at any time previous to your recent visit.

I see, says Jack.

No, you don't, says Mary Smith. Yes, I do, says Jack. No, Jack, I'm sure you don't, says Mary Smith. Yes, Mary Smith, I'm sure I do, says Jack.

It's your heart, Jack! It's your heart! says Mary Smith, pulling from the black plastic bag, the small black, heart-shaped bottle. You left your heart in our apartment, and now I have brought it back to you!

Don't be silly, says Jack, that's my grandfather's special hooch. Excuse me? says Mary Smith.

My grandfather was an explorer, says Jack, and in his explorations, he penetrated the most obscure and distant regions. I see, says Mary Smith. No, you don't, says Jack. It was an arduous occupation with hazards all its own. I remember as a small child noticing a pattern marking his visits to the house of my father, my mother and I. Your father? says Mary Smith. An unregenerate ne'er-do-well, says Jack. I'm sorry, says Mary Smith. It's all right, says

Jack. We weren't close. I understand, says Mary Smith. How can you? says Jack.

Your grandfather? says Mary Smith. A pattern, says Jack. He visited us sporadically in his later years, and when he visited he always brought with him the very bottle you are now holding in your hand. Oh, says Mary Smith. It grew, says Jack, in increments. That's revolting! says Mary Smith.

What I mean is the quantity of liquid in that bottle increased each time he visited us, says Jack. I remember distinctly one morning when, after rapping repeatedly on the tin door of our domicile, he was admitted in his tan explorer's outfit, and he sat on our ragged couch, and pulled from his rucksack that very bottle. Ahhh, says Mary Smith.

That's just what he said, says Jack. Ahhh...you boys! my grandfather said—holding that bottle in front of his face with one hand and fumbling for his explorer's monocle with the other—could never imagine the sublime and horrible vistas I have endured in my long wanderings among obscure and distant regions. Your frail and tiny brains are incapable of grasping such devastating impressions and were your brains to have those impressions thrust upon them, it's my guess they would crack. Crack? says Mary Smith. Be rent asunder, says Jack. Right, says Mary Smith.

He wasn't kidding, says Jack, and he knew what he was talking about. He had "been there" so to speak. I see, says Mary Smith. No, you don't says Jack. None of us did. None of us ever became privy to those devastating impressions, and my grandfather, poor soul, could only bring himself to speak of them in the vaguest terms possible. A pattern? says Mary Smith.

As the quantity of liquid in that bottle increased in increments with each of my grandfather's visits, so too did the stature of my grandfather decrease in increments, says Jack. And although these increments were small at first, later they were very much larger and completely out of proportion to the increments of increase I observed in the black liquid in that bottle. In the end my grandfather was reduced to the size of a very small dot and then disappeared altogether, leaving me with that bottle of hooch which I had planned on sharing with you and your better half, Parson Smith.

How do you know it's special hooch? says Mary Smith. And not say an extremely concentrated distillation of the horrors your grandfather witnessed in his travels? It's gotta be hooch, says Jack. Would you care to share some with me now? I don't know, says Mary Smith. Perhaps we should call your better half, Parson Smith, says Jack. Perhaps he would enjoy an impromptu late night gathering around a bottle of my grandfather's special hooch.

The bottle feels inordinately warm, says Mary Smith. A good deal warmer, in fact, than room temperature, which in our present circumstances feels quite high already. Would you mind opening that large picture window at the front of this room? It doesn't open, says Jack. I've tried it. Are you sure? says Mary Smith.

It used to open, I think, says Jack, but it doesn't open anymore. On hot summer nights I used to lie right over there on the floor bathed in moonlight and breezes, I think. But I don't anymore. More recently I've sweltered, sleepless and sweating for hours with no wish more ardent in my breast than the opening of that large picture window, but it doesn't open. You can pull and pull and weep and pull and pull some more. It simply doesn't open. Someone painted it shut.

Besides, says Jack, unscrewing the cap. Special hooch is always warmer than room temperature.

How about this, says Mary Smith. Just suppose that in his travels to obscure and distant regions, your grandfather had the ill luck of repeatedly encountering noxious animals of the domestic but undomesticated variety. The fragrance is enlightening without approaching boorishness, wouldn't you agree? says Jack. And suppose, says Mary Smith, your grandfather found it necessary to procure an appropriate remedy to such infestations.

You might say, says Jack, that it cuddles the olfactories without bruising them.

The kind of remedy I am speaking of, Jack, says Mary Smith, would quickly, silently and effectively perform its function, requiring your grandfather only to collect the corpses of the aforementioned beasts afterwards. Rat poison? says Jack. Exactly, says Mary Smith.

There is a small conflagration under Mary Smith's nighty.

No, says Jack, pouring dollops of the thick black liquid into their glasses. My dad told me. Jack tosses his shot back without putting down the bottle. Oh boy! says Jack.

Your dad? says Mary Smith. My dad, says Jack, whose name was also Jack, took me on his knee shortly after the infinite diminution of my grandfather and explained it to me. He said, I don't know where the old guy got it or what its constituent ingredients might be, but you can tell its damn fine hooch just by looking at it, can't you, Little Jack?

Little Jack is Little Jack! says Little Jack, says the little guy.

Oh dear, says Mary Smith, tossing back her shot.

Let me take care of that for you, says Jack, dropping to his knees in front of Mary Smith. Oh be gentle, good Jack, says Mary Smith, whose pupils have rolled up into her head.

Parson Smith is Parson Smith. Jack is Jack. My mother and my father won't come back. A room is a room and a rat is a rat. Pull up my nighty and hooray for Little Jack!

There is no such person, says Jack, and he plunges under Mary Smith's nighty.

A struggle ensues.

There is a knock at the door.

I know you're up here, you good for nothing bitch! says a voice behind the door. You think I'm blind, don't you? You think I'm the bland sort who wouldn't notice or might notice but passively condone your intrigues and carryings on with any ne'er-do-well willing to haul his carcass into our domicile, swill our hooch and patronize your ludicrous fantasies!

Oh dear, says Mary Smith, coming out of her swoon. It'll take just another minute, says Jack. C'mon out here little guy. THE RATS ARE COMING FOR LITTLE JACK!!! SAYS LITTLE JACK, says the little guy.

Shameless hussy! says the voice behind the door.
Brazen strumpet! You thought I was sleeping,
didn't you? You though you could slip out
unobserved and perform perverse gyrations with
that hooch swilling bastard, didn't you? You were
wrong!

Who is it? Mary Smith calls from the couch.

I got you now, little guy! says Jack, whose legs are
now splayed against the couch for leverage.

You would say you don't know me?!? says the
voice.

Are you from the hooch depot? says Mary Smith.

There is a loud bumping against the door. The door
bellies out. Wisps of dust escape the frame.

Jack, says Mary Smith, I think there's someone at
the door for you. Heaugh! says Jack, Heaugh!
Heaugh! Heaugh!

The door to Jack's room cracks off its hinges and
drops flat on the floor. The body of Parson Smith
fills the door frame.

Parson Smith! says Mary Smith. Mary Smith! says
Parson Smith.

A loud wet sound is emitted from underneath the nighty of Mary Smith. Jack falls backward with a dripping, roughly spherical object in his hands. The object is a head.

The eyes in the head open, blink away the drippings that have gotten into them and irritably survey the room.

Little Jack is Little Jack, says the head of Little Jack.

Now the time has grown early. The sun's flushed face bobs up among the buildings. The light from that sun slides through the big front window of Jack's room. As that light slides through that window, it is shaved into long planks which bend and warp around the contorted bodies of Parson Smith, Mary Smith and Jack.

The Rats: Of course we arrived on the scene at the appointed time. Agents had had the building under surveillance from early on in the evening. There was a minor breach of cover involving premature communication with the client, Parson Smith, but otherwise all proceeded smoothly. Our operatives succeeded in establishing secure posts at the kitchen window and all clandestine and aquatic access points to Jack's room well before the go moment, and when that moment came, were ready to proceed with a high degree of dispatch. This we did, swarming into the room simultaneously from all access points, taking maximum advantage of surprise and completely paralyzing the enemy's capacity for counter measures. Indeed, the effectiveness of this piece of flawlessly executed shock tactics far exceeded our expectations, significantly destabilizing "Jack"—who subsequently departed the scene in a state of extreme confusion, if not hysteria, and has since been spotted raving in the streets—and reducing "Mary Smith" to a state of catatonia which we have good reason to believe will prove permanent. The friendly, client Parson Smith, was not collaterally affected, and we believe we can rely on his usefulness in the future with a high degree of confidence. From an operational standpoint, it is fair to call this sortie a complete success and we recommend the highest commendations to all involved. The loss of the Little Jack's head is of course regrettable, but we do not believe that loss can be attributed to any error in planning or execution. Indeed, we had foreseen the possibility of decapitation as an operational contingency as well as the projection of the aforementioned head through and out the front window by "Jack." Though we have yet to locate the head, we have every reason to expect that it will soon be found, bearing out our tried and true motto, "We take what falls."

The doctor: Heads that are not attached to bodies should be and remain silent not only because that is in accordance with all that is reasonable, natural and scientific but also because it is only proper, polite and indeed moral that they do so. That the head spoke in a complete and grammatically correct sentence we can only regard as an insult to our already injured sensibility, and as such not worthy of further comment.

Henry: From the overly large and long hands of Jack—did you know his hands are large? How has this fact gone unreported? For they are large, and long. If you stared at his fingers, you would see that they go on for miles. I can feel myself slipping—the head of Little Jack, for he is no other, shot through the glass of Jack's large front window and it was at that moment—while Jack remained oblivious to the swarm of rodents that had converged under the nighty of Mary Smith to devour the truncated body of Little Jack, for he is no other—that Jack lost his senses. The glass, of course, shattered. It shattered into an infinity of shards, some as fine as snow and some as gross as slivers of stone. Powdered glass was also emitted in cloudlets which rained themselves to the floor in tiny strings. It was this shattering that effected his madness. For there is nothing as irrevocable as a shattered window.

The Magnate: After the head had pierced that sad soul's window, it should have gone down like this. It should have gone down just like this—in a parabolic curve negotiating the dispute between its forward acceleration and the immense sucking of our green planet. It should have gone down like this to the ground, and if it found pavement there without purchase, woe unto it, for that is barren land where nothing is given leave to grow. But, if it found soft black earth in which to embed itself as a seed is embedded, then Lo! Rejoice! For a tree shall grow there, and unto that tree shall fruit be given.

Ralph: The head went up.

Henry: A slide, a slip, a crack. Everything settles. Down. The foundation gives its weight to the mud. A sinking, planks break. There's no clearing it. There's no upward going. In and down, through mud ribboned with cold wet. All those bricks are above, pulled apart. They wander with tons above them, tons that are miles. How many places are there to go in this no place? Dirt in the nostrils, in the ear canals, in the throat, in the anus: envelope of shit, alimentary canal...

Jack:

The perfunctory little man behind the desk: Jack, I'm your little man. How are you?
Jack: I've been better.
The little man: Not really.
Jack: It's a manner of speaking.
The little man: We are not speaking right now, Jack. We have never spoken. We don't speak. We will never speak.
Jack:
The little man: Now, I'm going to tell you the story of the little no-man in the little no-man's land. He lived with a little no-woman and a no-dog. The no-woman pulled open her long incision. Are you listening, Jack?
Jack:
The little man: The no-woman pulled open her long incision. The no-man pulled open his long incision. The no-dog stood up on its hind legs to watch them. Are you listening, Jack?
Jack:
The little man: The no-dog stood up on its hind legs to watch them with their incisions pulled open. The no-dog opened its muzzle. The no-dog began its no-dog declamation. Are you listening, Jack?
Jack:
The little man: The no-dog began. The no-dog, up on its hind legs, gestured with its forepaws, which were pellet shaped and black like briquettes of

charcoal. That was the manner of the no-dog. And this is its declamation.

The no-dog: In another place, the moon's bright white face grimaced up beyond the high hill. It grimaced and grunted, and its white face was stretched back toward the high hill. A no-dog watched the struggle of the white faced moon from the other place and this place was far, far away. This no-dog, who was not myself, watched the struggle of the white faced moon, and this no-dog, distinct from myself, declaimed. This is the declamation of the no-dog who is not myself: Where is the no-man? Where is the no-woman? There is no-one to see the fine white moon with its face stretched back toward the high hill. There is no-one but the no-dog, and this no-dog is myself.

This is absolutely true, says Mona to the ne'er-do-well seated at a small table in the pit beside the stage. This guy said, Come with me. We'll go to my place and have a good time there. So, I got into his car, which wasn't a great car but more of an all right car, and his car putted through the streets, and the streets were empty and streaked with neon in their puddles. And soon enough—though it took longer than I had expected—we arrived at his place, and he got out of the car and opened the car door for me. And I got out too and followed him through the sounds and smells of the building up the steps to the floor where his room was.

One of the floors in that building on the street near the old warehouse and the old factory? says the ne'er-do-well. Exactly, says Mona. I was there once, says the ne'er-do-well, on business. I was drunk, says Mona. I'd been drinking hooch all night. The guy bought it for me. Sap, says the ne'er-do-well. No, says Mona, he wasn't.

It took us forever to get up those steps, says Mona. I mean that literally. And when we got to the door to his room, we were both out of breath and we stood up there for a while, panting at each other. Oh Mona baby! says the ne'er-do-well. No, says Mona, just panting. And he pulled his key ring out of his trouser pocket and opened the door. It took him forever to unlock the door because he was pretty drunk too, says Mona. I mean that literally. And he was playing with his trousers at the same time. That guy was a pervert, says the ne'er-do-well.

No, says Mona, he wasn't. He worked at the hooch depot. He was steady. He was O.K. Sure baby, says the ne'er-do-well. His room was a shitty little room but it was well kept except for all the newspapers, says Mona. It surprised me that there were also plants in the room and all these plants were green and living though some them were yellow in places. The ne'er-do-well rolls his eyes up at Mona to indicate that he doubts the accuracy of what she is telling him. But what surprised me more, baby, says Mona, was that there was a woman all tied up, crouching in the corner of the room. Whoa! says the ne'er-do-well. She was wearing a dirty white nighty, says Mona, and her name was Mary Smith.

That's Mary Smith, the guy said, says Mona. I found her in a crumpled heap way out in the huge lot behind the big building in which conventions are sometimes held. She was in a crumpled heap, wearing the very same nighty she is wearing now. She asked me to tie her up, the guy said. I wouldn't do that on my own initiative. I don't want you to tie me up, I said, says Mona. Oh baby! says the ne'er-do-well.

No, says Mona, I really didn't. In fact, as far as I can recall, I've never wanted anyone to tie me up. That's not to say I have never allowed anyone to tie me up. I have. Oh baby! says the ne'er-do-well. But that was only a specific incident which occurred under very exceptional circumstances, says Mona. O.K., says the ne'er-do-well. Then the guy walked over to where Mary Smith was crouching and removed the gag she had been chewing on. Why don't you talk to Mary Smith while I get something out of the fridge, the guy said.

So I went and sat in a wicker chair near the corner where Mary Smith was crouching. Only now she wasn't just crouching, she was crouching and clearing her throat. Oh ba—says the ne'er-do-well. Shut up! says Mona. That's becoming annoying. Kay, says the ne'er-do-well.

Do you think, says Mona, that it's significant that the chair I was sitting in was made out of wicker?

Rattan. Most of those chairs are made out of rattan, says the ne'er-do-well. In fact, when I visited the building you are speaking of, I believe I sold several chairs and if I remember correctly, they were all made out of rattan, says the ne'er-do-well, who has shiny black hair and an earring with a stone in it.

Oh, says Mona, fastening the buckle which is on the front of her red brassiere. Would you like to take me to your table back there and buy me drinks? Sure, says the ne'er-do-well. They have a two-for special at this establishment, and I would be pleased if you would drink the second drink I receive with each first drink I order. Fair enough, says Mona, pulling red panties up along her long slender legs. And she ducks under the chrome railing around the stage, steps down and takes the ne'er-do-well's hand in her own and leads him to a small round table on a raised area of the floor in back. Is hooch O.K. ? says the ne'er-do-well. It's all they have, says Mona. I have noticed that, says the ne'er-do-well, opening and closing his hand rapidly near the edge of the table.

An unremarkable girl in a short skirt brings them two small juice glasses filled with hooch and ice. And that's for you, says the ne'er-do-well, pressing an extra bill into the soft palm of the unremarkable girl. You are quite a guy, Henry, the unremarkable girl says. Henry rolls his eyes at Mona to indicate that he doubts the sincerity of what the unremarkable girl has said. Here's to ya, says Mona, downing all the hooch in one swallow. Reciprocally, says Henry, doing the same.

When Mary Smith finished clearing her throat, says Mona, she started talking. She said, says Mona, Oh Mona! It's been so long since I've seen you. So long. That is, such a long time. It's been such a long time that now I am not at all sure that I have seen you. I have seen you, haven't I? I have seen and conversed with you, haven't I? Or is it possible that I've only heard about you? Perhaps from my former better half Parson Smith? Perhaps it was he that conversed with you, not I, and it was I that only heard about you from him. You have conversed with my former better half, Parson Smith, haven't you? Parson who? I said. Smith, said Mary Smith, Parson Smith. No, I don't believe so, I said, says Mona.

That was true. I don't believe I had ever conversed with Parson Smith though I had met him. But that was in a very unusual and fleeting circumstance, and I didn't think it bore mentioning to Mary Smith within the circumstances I was then encountering her. I have conversed with Parson Smith, says Henry. It was at a convention. I thought he was a worthy sort of unusual abilities. But there was something about him. Yes, says Mona, even in the fleeting circumstances when I met him, I too noticed that there was something about him. He was marked, says Henry. Exactly, says Mona. But Mary Smith was unmarked, says Henry. Notably unmarked, says Mona.

Mary Smith then said, says Mona—her pale cheeks flushing red as the hooch dilates the fine net of capillaries within them. If I haven't met you before, then certainly now I am meeting you for the first time, and if that is the case, I am pained and saddened. I am sure that if we had met under more convivial circumstances, we would have hit it off immediately and become fast friends in the time it would have take to while away the afternoon. Well... , I said, says Mona. But as it is, said Mary Smith, I'm afraid that after you have accomplished whatever purpose has brought you to this squalid room with newspapers and plants, you will leave without a thought of me in your head, beyond a receding curiosity and if we are to meet again, it will have to be by chance.

Ah yes, says Henry, it's often like that. For you maybe, says Mona. But I didn't have the foggiest notion of what she was talking about. I didn't have any purpose in coming to that squalid room in the first place. I was, so to speak, says Mona, winging it. I see, says Henry.

But before you go, said Mary Smith, says Mona, I must relate to you my journey through the air and how I came to undertake it, for that journey was miraculous and I have reason to believe, universally instructive. Well..., I said and I looked across the squalid room to the doorway of the kitchen which glowed yellow because there was a light on in there. And I could hear the guy who had brought me shuffling about, but unfortunately there was no sign of his imminent return.

It was miraculous, said Mary Smith. I have already related it to the proprietor of this squalid room, and he was acutely interested and agreed wholeheartedly that the journey was miraculous and well worth hearing about. Well..., I said again, and looked toward the kitchen again, again hoping that there would be some sign of the guy's imminent return; perhaps the appearance of his ungainly figure limned with yellow in the door frame, for example...

No dice? says Henry.

It all began, said Mary Smith, says Mona, because of an unfortunate accident involving myself, my former better half, Parson Smith, an acquaintance of ours named Jack, some rats and a small child. Jack? I said. You know him? said Mary Smith. Never heard of him, I said, says Mona.

You've never met Jack? says Henry. In my line of work, says Mona. You meet a lot of both savory and unsavory character, if you know what I mean. Uh yeah, says Henry. And it is not the least bit unusual, says Mona, for one or several of these characters to develop an unhealthy fixation on one's person without the tiniest bit of encouragement from oneself beyond what is customary and commercially necessary in an establishment such as this. I get you, says Henry.

Misunderstandings naturally arise, says Mona, and sometimes these misunderstandings can become elaborate, protracted and involved. Of course from a commercial standpoint, that's not always such a bad thing, but from a personal standpoint, it is frequently disastrous or worse. Right, says Henry, I think something like that happened to a friend of mine.

That's why a woman in my position has to keep on her toes, says Mona. Mentally, that is. And no matter how elaborate, protracted and involved a misunderstanding becomes in the mind of an afflicted client and no matter how elaborately a woman in my position has accommodated herself to that misunderstanding; it is crucial that she keep clear in her mind the line, often no thicker than a hair, separating the true and natural state of affairs from the sick amalgamation of lusts and fantasy that has grown up around it.

More hooch? says Henry, drawing out his wallet. Certainly, says Mona.

The details of that accident escape me completely now, said Mary Smith, says Mona, but its consequences I remember vividly and exactly. Oh? I said, to be polite.

I became immersed, said Mary Smith, in a state of great clarity. I see, I said. No you don't, said Mary Smith. How could you? How could my former better half Parson Smith see? How could the doctor who completed my therapy see? No one could see, Mona, said Mary Smith, adopting a tone of confidentiality with which I was not altogether comfortable.

In fact, no one saw anything, said Mary Smith. It was I that saw everything, and they that saw nothing even though my former better half and the doctor were both convinced of the reverse. They thought they saw everything and I saw nothing. Nothing could have been further from the truth, Mona, said

Mary Smith. And y'know I really didn't like it when she called me Mona, says Mona. In fact, it kinda gave me the creeps. Overly familiar? says Henry. Maybe, says Mona.

You see, said Mary Smith, immediately after that accident which plunged me into a state of great clarity, my former better half, Parson Smith, dragged me down. He dragged me down from the high room where we had all been. He dragged me down from that high room which had become crowded with tattered breezes, streaming and shredding in over the sharp edges of the broken window. He dragged me down from there to our own squalid domicile, and it was evident from his posture and attitude toward me how thoroughly he had misapprehended my situation. It was evident that he thought I had become immersed in a state of great obscurity, but as I have told you, precisely the opposite was the case.

I didn't help him drag me, but neither did I hinder him. It was not my business to help or hinder. It was my business to be dragged, and I understood this absolutely.

He dragged me down, whispering consoling nonsense in my ear, but when he got me back into our room, his attitude changed completely. He became aggressive and hostile in a way that I had seen before but to a degree with which I was unfamiliar. It was clear that he wished for a vigorous response from me to his aggression and hostility, but it was not my business to respond. It was only my business to watch him and be supremely cognizant, and this is exactly what I did. Of course this lack of response coupled with my supreme cognizance, which of course he mistook for supreme ignorance, only inflamed him further until he was quite beside himself. I mean that literally.

He was beside himself. That is a Parson Smith-shaped thing stood beside my former better half, Parson Smith, and the two of them together vented the rage of my former better half, Parson Smith, by encasing me in a bulky, many buckled apparatus with which I was not unfamiliar, and performing various gross and minute ministrations on my person. These ministrations went on for sometime—and I assure you I remember each one exactly though they were many and diverse—but finally the rage of Parson Smith had been vented and the two of them stopped, and sat on the couch together, talking.

As they were talking, nonsense I assure you, I was thinking. I was thinking how funny it was that they had encased me in the formidable apparatus to restrain me when, in fact, I required no restraint, but even if I had, I was not restrained such was the state of great clarity I had attained that restraint was completely out of the question. Have you ever felt that way, Mona? Have you ever found yourself in an extreme, or perhaps very mundane, situation and suddenly felt that restraint was completely out of the question? Well..., I said, says Mona, but I couldn't finish my sentence because I really had no idea of what to say as it was clear to me that the poor woman was completely out of her head. Obviously, says Henry, and yet... ?

Perhaps you have, said Mary Smith, says Mona, or perhaps you will. In any case that was how I felt, lying there in the apparatus, listening to my former better half, Parson Smith, talking to himself. They talked and talked. They talked through the remainder of the morning, well into the afternoon, and they continued into the evening and then talked all night. Finally my former better half, Parson Smith, had talked himself out, for the other was nowhere to be seen, and alone, he fell asleep. He slept as soundly as a babe, snoring all the while and his snores sounded just like a cello. A cello? say Henry. Deep and resonant, but mellow, says Mona. I see, says Henry. How can you? says Mona.

And then he woke up, said Mary Smith, says Mona. And his attitude had changed considerably. His aggression and hostility had been replaced with an almost touching solicitude and remorse directed at my person. But his attitude hadn't changed completely, for he persisted in misapprehending my state of mind as one of great obscurity where as I've said before, just the reverse was the case. Murmuring apologies and gentle solicitations, he rummaged in the closet for a while until he emerged with a little red wagon, into which he dragged and heaved my person which was still encased in the bulky apparatus. Wait a minute, I said, says Mona. Just how big was this wagon?

You see, says Mona, It had suddenly occurred to me that perhaps Mary Smith was not as out of her head as she seemed. It occurred to me that perhaps she was not only as sane as you or I, but also wily, and in her wiliness, she had been pulling my leg all along, perhaps with the complicity of the guy who had brought me there.

That guy was ungainly, right? says Henry.   Yeah, says Mona.   He had the look of a twit about him, right? says Henry. Well—says Mona. I know that guy, says Henry.

He is wily. When I was at the building you've been speaking of, I believe I sold that very same guy a rattan chair under the pretense that it was wicker. I got a very good price for it from him and to all appearances, it seemed I had got the better of him. But just as I was climbing back into the cab with his and other's money in my pocket, feeling pleased and successful, that guy—it must have been him, a kind of long head and with the look of a twit about him—came rushing out of the building and over to my car. I thought he'd figured out that his chair was rattan and was going to demand his money back. In fact, by the time he got to the car, I'd already taken his money out of my pocket. But he didn't want it back. He just stuck his head in the car window, took my hands in his own, and a little tearfully, thanked me for the chair. He really laid on the gratitude. So much so that as the cab was pulling away and I could see that twitty looking ungainly guy in the review mirror, standing on the curb, still waving good bye, I couldn't help feeling that somehow he'd put one over on me, but that I wouldn't discover exactly what he'd done for some time.

It's the same guy, says Mona.

When I said "little red wagon," said Mary Smith, says Mona. I was referring to the type of wagon rather than its size. In fact, it was a fairly large little red wagon, even very large, as my entire frame and the bulky apparatus in which it was encased fit neatly inside. Moreover, it was such a large little red wagon, I felt like a tiny girl riding inside it, and my former better half, Parson Smith, pulling it, appeared no bigger than a toddler with the wagon's big black handle stuck under his arm. But pull he did. Out of our squalid domicile, down two short flights of steps, through the vestibule of our building, and out the front door to the sidewalk where he kept pulling the wagon with me in it all the way across town.

Were you mortified? I asked, says Mona. Because I certainly would have been. No, said Mary Smith, I remained in a state of great clarity which did not allow for mortification even though I was fully cognizant that the two of us, fully grown, rolling along sidewalks and bumping down curbs with that grotesquely oversized wagon made a pitiful and mortifying sight indeed. Certainly, if I hadn't been immersed in a state of great clarity, I would have been mortified and that mortification would have increased geometrically as each ne'er-do-well we passed responded to the pathos of our condition by tossing a coin or in some cases several coins, into the wagon where I lay. In fact, so many coins were tossed into the wagon that by the time we reached the doctor's office somewhere in the big building in which conventions are sometimes held, it looked as if I, encased in the apparatus, were lying on a pallet of silver, whose silver stuffing nearly overflowed the sides of the wagon.

That's a lot of change, I said, says Mona. Yes, said Mary Smith, it was. And it impressed the doctor too when we finally reached him in his stiflingly small office somewhere deep inside the big building in which conventions are sometimes held. That's a lot of change, he said, as soon as we had finished bumping through the doorway into his office. But my former better half, who had drawn on even more of the garments of remorse during our journey—in fact he had become quite bundled in them—was all business. He didn't respond to the doctor's remark, but pointed immediately at me, still under the misconception that I had been plunged into a state of great obscurity, and said,

Something needs to be done, and the doctor answered, No kidding.

Let's see, said the doctor, and he scratched his chin as if he had a beard, which in fact, he didn't have. Actually, he appeared rather youthful, if not juvenile, sitting as he was on the examination table with his short legs dangling over the edge. In fact he looked less like a doctor and more like a child dressed in the guise of a doctor for a show of some sort or grade school pageant.

Let's see, the doctor said again, hopping off the table and gaining considerably in stature. Let's see, he said a third time and he began to examine my person minutely—that is the portions of my person not obscured by the apparatus, that is my face—while my former better half, Parson Smith, stood dumbly on the side with a look of great and touching concern spread across his features.

I confess I thought they appeared rather funny there in that little room, adopting postures of consultation and concern about what exactly needed to be done. For I, immersed as I was in a state of great clarity, knew with absolute certainty that nothing needed to be done, nothing at all. But I didn't say anything. It was not for me to disabuse them of their misconceptions. It was for me to be silent and watch in an attitude of supreme cognizance as if it were a puppet show I were watching.

How long has she been this way? said the doctor. Are you sure you're a doctor? said my better half, Parson Smith, who had become canny during the examination.

Oh boy, said the doctor, jumping back up on the examination table and allowing his legs to resume their dangling. I am precisely not sure. I know that when I started working here, I really and dearly wanted to be a doctor. And I know that since then, I have felt qualified and able to be a doctor. And recently I have become sure that I have the full confidence of the staff due to their oft-stated conviction that if I were not a doctor already, I would soon be made one...

Is this your name here? interrupted my former better half, pulling a card from his pocket. Yes! said the doctor, hopping smartly off the table and regaining his full stature. She's been like this for some time, said Parson Smith.

Ahh... yes, said the doctor.

There was this accident involving me, Jack, our neighbor, my better half, Mary Smith here, some rats and a small child, said Parson Smith. Hmm... , said the doctor. Shortly after that accident, said Parson Smith, and after I had managed to wrestle my better half, Mary Smith here, back into our cozy domicile and into the therapeutic apparatus in which she is presently encased, I and a very close friend of mine, who is and shall remain nameless, performed various and minute ministrations on her person. Ministrations? said the doctor.

I confess, said my former better half, I was extremely agitated, if not angry while we were performing these ministrations. Do you think that was wrong? Do you think it was wrong of me to perform those ministrations in an agitated if not angry state? Normally, said the doctor. Normally? said my former better half. Yes, said the doctor. What? said my former better half. Normally, yes, said the doctor. We have reached an impasse, said my former better half who had become confused. It would have been wrong of you under normal circumstances, said the doctor. Oh, said my former better half.

But worry not, good Parson, said the doctor. While we have been standing here prattling on about nothing, a different, more acute region of my brain has been vigorously engaging the problem at hand, and I have devised a therapy. Thank goodness, said Parson Smith. Let's go outside, said the doctor. There is a piece of equipment in the lot behind this building, which I believe should suit our purposes admirably though when you see it, you'll realize it was designed for altogether different purposes.

The doctor then led my better half, who pulled me in the little red wagon behind him, out of the small office, into a short and narrow hallway, which shortly turned into a long and wide hallway, to a door which opened on a staircase. We bumped down several flights of stairs—more flights, if I remember correctly, than we had ascended to reach the doctor's office—until we came to the bottom at which there was a very small door without a doorknob and that door was painted green.

Here we are, said the doctor, said Mary Smith, says Mona, and he opened that small green door without a door knob by pushing it hard with the heel of his hand, and as the door swung open, the largest, brownest and emptiest lot imaginable was revealed beyond it.

It was a very empty lot but not completely empty for some distance from where we had emerged, a very large and ramshackle device sloped darkly against the pale yellow sky.

Either this lot behind the big building in which conventions are sometimes held is actually much larger than one could have expected from viewing the front of the building, said my former better half, Parson Smith, or it has been painstakingly and meticulously landscaped such that, by rising subtly as it stretches away from the building, it merely gives one the impression that it reaches all the way to the horizon. Very astute! said the doctor. Let's go!

He took off like a shot into the immense and immensely, but not completely, empty lot. My former better half hurried to follow him with the handle of the wagon still under his arm, and I, behind him, encased and supine on a bed of silver, jerked and bumped over the uneven ground.

On we went. The doctor, in his white lab coat, flitted and darted in front like a moth. Parson Smith trudged and trudged, and I bumped and bumped. After we had gone some distance, my former better half began to tire somewhat and in his fatigue, he started to puff and wheeze in a repulsive fashion. His puffing and wheezing was repulsive but this repulsiveness did not penetrate the serenity with which I was enshrouded, immersed as I was in a state of great clarity, for that serenity was impregnable in every way. As we drew closer to the device, its dark whole began to resolve itself into constituent parts and soon I was able to clearly make out a tree trunk, a ramshackle carriage, a cup shaped protrusion and a large rock. My better half Parson Smith could see them too, for upon seeing them he took heart, and as he took heart he whistled.

Stop! says Henry. That's it!

It was at a convention that I met Parson Smith. And I can tell you authoritatively that his better half was pulling your leg there when she said he whistled, says Henry. Huh? says Mona. If I remember

correctly, says Henry, at that convention—which
was for parsons as well as men in my line of work,
though we were never officially invited—one night,
some of the guys got together for a whistling contest
just to horse around and pass the time. And if my
memory serves me right, that Parson Smith was a
real king loser when it came to whistling. He'd just
blow and blow and blow but nothing ever came out
but little bits of spit and air. But what was worse
was that he seemed ashamed of this incapacity, and
kept insisting that he could do it but was just having
an off day. It was embarrassing. Who won? says
Mona. Some ne'er-do-well who'd crashed the
convention for free hooch. His name was Jack, I
believe, says Henry. Jack? says Mona. You know
him? says Henry. Never heard of him, says Mona.

Here's your hooch, says the unremarkable girl, who
is, as it turns out, not completely unremarkable but
rather horse-faced.

He whistled a lengthy tune, said Mary Smith, says
Mona, tossing back all her hooch in one gulp. And
when he came to the end of it, he whistled it again.
He whistled the tune three times, but the device on
the horizon didn't appear to get any closer. I began
to fear that we would never reach it at all but be
caught eternally approaching it when suddenly we
were there.

The shadow of the device fell blackly across the still
flitting form of the doctor, my exhausted former

better half, and myself still supine and serene in the wagon.

I have to confess, said the doctor gleefully capering around the device, that although my primary motive in applying this particular therapy to your better half is of course to see her condition improved, I am also strongly moved by a desire to test out the therapy I have devised in my mind in actualis mundi, so to speak. Do you think that's wrong of me?

It looks like a catapult, said my better half, of the kind once used to assault medieval fortresses.

And he was right, said Mary Smith, says Mona. For the device had an arm made of a thick tree trunk which was bent to the ground, just like a catapult's, and a cup shaped protrusion at the end of that arm, just like the cup at the end of the arm of a catapult, and inside that cup, nestled a boulder, just as a boulder might nestle in the cup of a catapult. Moreover, the cup was fastened to the ground by ropes which were tied to thick stakes and beside these stakes lay a sharp knife, glittering.

If you will assist the patient in mounting the projectile, said the doctor, we can begin the treatment, which is very quick in its application but will be, I believe, long lasting in its effects. I don't know, said my former better half, who was a bit taken a back. Er ger erger erger, I said, in an effort to express my delight for, in as much as my state of great clarity allowed for it, I was delighted.

Let me help you, said the doctor, who then dragged me, not without difficulty, by the apparatus onto the boulder to which he secured me, facing out, with a roll of strong white surgical tape which he had pulled from his pocket. I did not assist the doctor. Nor did I resist him, as it was not for me to assist or resist. It was for me to remain supple but unmoving in a state of great clarity and delight which I would have gladly expressed at the top of my lungs were there any call to do so which, of course, there was none.

That should do the trick, said the doctor when he had finished. Do you feel better honey? said my former better half, standing on tip-toes beside the rock so that he could speak in my ear.

And I was very pleased he did that for that was the last time I saw him and I feel certain now that I shall never see him again. And so, I am very pleased that it is in that rising and supplicating posture, with those sweet words of concern on his lips that I shall always remember him, said Mary Smith.

Sure, baby, sure, I said, trying to be kind, but she didn't notice my kindness at all. She just looked at me with her black limpid eyes, which widened momentarily, and then she resumed chewing on the gag. For the guy who had brought me there had returned quietly from the kitchen and slipped the gag back into her mouth.

Whoa boy! says Henry. That Mary Smith, she's quite a number ain't she? You're a pig, says Mona, and you haven't been listening to a word I've been saying. Well, says Henry. And I haven't even gotten to the most interesting part yet, says Mona. Well, says Henry.

Mary Smith's eyes did not widen in response to the imminent replacement of her gag as you may have supposed, says Mona. No, it wasn't that that caused her eyes which were as black as buttons to widen. In fact, I think as far as the gag was concerned, she was grateful, for she sighed contentedly, I thought, when it was slipped back into her mouth, and the chewing she resumed was a contented chewing, I thought. No, the gag was less a problem for her than a solution. Her eyes widened because when the guy returned he did not return unencumbered but was carrying a large metal bowl with him and this large metal bowl was covered by a piece of cheese cloth. The guy set the bowl on a table near the door, and Mary Smith's eyes widened when she saw it, and her gaze never left that bowl for all of the remaining time I was there.

Do you think, says Mona, that it is significant that the large metal bowl was covered with cheese cloth? It could breathe, says Henry. Breathe? says Mona. If, for example, there was a large twist of bread dough nestled in the bottom of that metal bowl, says Henry, the weave of the cheese cloth would allow that dough to breathe. That is macabre, says Mona.

Not at all, says Henry. Bread dough generally contains live yeast cultures which produce certain gases as a result of the process of cellular respiration. It is these gases that infiltrate the bread dough causing it to rise into the soft fluffy loaves we all know well and consume. Oh, says Mona. I say that of course, only in reference to leavened bread, says Henry. In the case of unleavened bread, which the Jews call Matzo, that process is retarded or passed over all together. I have dealt in both leavened and unleavened bread, says Henry.

Would you like to take me back to your place of residence? says Mona. I live in a hotel, says Henry. That's all right by me, says Mona. I'll call a cab, says Henry. I'll get dressed, says Mona.

The city is dripping and oozing outside. Henry stands under the maroon awning in front of the establishment, listening to the drips and oozes. After a while, Mona comes out and stands beside him. The manner in which she comes out is one of "flouncing." Mona comes flouncing out and stands beside Henry, her oversized furry purse bouncing against her hip. The cab will be here soon, says Henry. Here it is, says Mona.

The cab slides along the wet street and up to the curb. The cab is yellow. The cab is also streaked with dirt and bits of things. The front window of the cab moves down in jerks and starts. The cabby sticks his face into the opening. The cabby's face is encumbered with a large red nose and large bloodshot green eyes. Henry? the cabby says.

Inside the establishment, the girls are still dancing and chatting up the ne'er-do-wells. Some ne'er-do-wells are watching with fascinated curiosity. Other are watching with dull lust. Still other ne'er-do-wells are sleeping with their cheeks against the table tops, and just dreaming about girls in an establishment like this one. A certain example of a fourth type of ne'er-do-well is standing in the men's room looking at the short thick black hairs in his nostrils in the men's room mirror. A few moments later, he is looking at the colorful labels lined up vertically on a white metal box of condoms mounted on the wall. Outside, the not completely unremarkable but rather horse-faced girl is couching behind the bar out of sight, having a cigarette. She is thinking about her mother. She is thinking, My mother might have at one time found herself crouching behind the bar at a certain establishment like this one, thinking about her mother, but she never would have told me about it. She would have been wearing a cute hat, and that hat would have had feathers.

Close enough, says Henry, and he opens the passenger door of the car and slides in across the naugahyde seats. Mona slides in after him. The naugahyde seats are streaked with liquid. Some of this liquid is clear, and some of it is opaque. It doesn't stick, says the cabby over his shoulder through the open half of the plastic window above the back of the front seat. I clean up as best I can at night and in the morning, and often in between fares. We're going to a hotel, says Henry. He lives in a hotel, says Mona. Right, says the cabby and he slides the plastic window closed. The cab begins to move.

It wasn't bread in the large metal bowl which was covered with cheese cloth, says Mona, putting her hand on Henry's knee. Oh? says Henry. No, says Mona. It was some kind of liquid. I could hear it sloshing. Sloshing? says Henry. And I could see that in places the edges of the cheese cloth were sodden with liquid, and this liquid was brown and pink, says Mona, moving closer to Henry and letting her hand rest on the top part of the middle of his right leg.

A soup perhaps? Or a roast with some kind of gravy? says Henry. The guy set the bowl on the table near the door across from where Mary Smith crouched chewing on her gag, says Mona. She watched him do it. She watched him very carefully and when he had set the bowl on the table, she stopped chewing on her gag and just looked at the bowl. She looked at it with both her eyes. I have dealt in both soups and roasts, says Henry.

And then the guy said, says Mona, come over to my small table beside the door and have a glass of water with me. I would offer you hooch but I feel that if I consumed another drop of hooch, I might become ill, and I infer that a cognate disability afflicts you. He was right, says Mona. I'd already had about as much hooch as I could stand, and felt that if I consumed even a particle more, I would not only become ill but spew all over the newspapers littering the guy's shabby but otherwise well kept room.

Is your dwelling nearby? says Mona, looking past Henry out the window. Henry looks out the window too. The dirt and smears of mud and other bits of things obscure the view. Mona and Henry can only see one looming dark shape beside the road giving way to another looming dark shape. I think we're close, says Henry.

When we sat at the small table with the large metal bowl in the middle of it, Mona says, the guy poured some clear, cold water into a tall thin water glass which he handed to me over the metal bowl, and said, Mona, how long do you think time is? And I didn't know what to say. So he said, Some thinkers are of the opinion that time goes on and on and on and on and on like that forever. Ahh yes, I said, because I knew exactly what he meant. But there are other thinkers, he said, that think time goes on and on and on and on and on like that for a very long time and stops.

The cab slides to the curb. The cabby pulls the plastic window above the back of the front seat open and thrusts his face with its bloodshot eyes and enormous nose into the back seat. You're talking about the guy who works at the hooch depot, aren't you? the cabby says. Yes, says Mona. I know that guy, says the cabby. In what capacity? says Henry. This is your hotel, says the cabby. It's ten bucks. Right, says Henry and he pays the cabby, and he and Mona slide out of the cab, into the still dripping and oozing city night.

The cab goes away.

Mona and Henry are standing on the curb in front of the hotel. This hotel isn't a good hotel, but more of an all right hotel, says Henry. There was something about that cabby, says Mona. It was his nose, says Henry. Yes, says Mona. His nose. And she takes Henry's hand in her own, and he leads her around to the back of the hotel.

Your hair has become frosted with rain, says Henry, as they approach a short staircase near the pool. Yes, says Mona. It is very becoming here in the confused light of the courtyard behind this hotel, says Henry. Sure, says Mona. Especially when you stand in front of the shine-broken jade water of the swimming pool as you are now, says Henry. What are you getting at? says Mona.

My room is on the fifth floor, says Henry. All right, says Mona, and both at the same time, they mount the staircase.

So really, that's just about all there was to it, Mona says as they walk. That guy really put one over on me. I had come all the way to his crummy little room because he had promised me we'd have a good time but all we ended up doing was drinking water at this little table with a roast or something in a shiny metal bowl between us.

You were expecting something different, says Henry. I was expecting something more, says Mona. But after posing that rather odd question to me and answering it himself, the guy just became morose.

I think he had been morose all along, says Henry, who is breathing hard from walking up all those steps. Morose and wily. I think any previous shows of jollity he may have exhibited were forced and superficial, and that he habitually made gestures of that type as a kind of ruse, to obscure an essentially morose and morbid nature. You don't even know this guy, says Mona. I may have sold him a rattan chair, says Henry.

But even without knowing him, says Mona, you have, I believe, penetrated to the very core of his character. For sitting there at the small table with me, our two water glasses and the metal bowl, he demonstrated a moroseness of such unflagging persistence that it suggested to me that it indeed was more indicative of his inner nature than his hooch drinking, unerring sense of etiquette and domestic generosity, says Mona, between pants as they reach the third, the fourth or possibly the fifth landing.

How so? says Henry between heaves of labored breathing. Just a second, says Mona, who is breathing too heavily to talk. Oh god, says Mona leaning back against the short railing that skirts the landing. This may be my floor, says Henry, finally. But I'm not sure because I haven't been counting, and all the floors in this hotel look disconcertingly alike. I have noticed that, says Mona.

A tall elderly man in a white bathrobe walks past them toward the stairs. He is carrying an empty white plastic ice bucket. Is this the fourth floor? Henry calls to him as he passes. No, the elderly man says without looking back. It must be the fifth then, says Henry to Mona, because I'm sure we've walked up more than three flights.

Because he didn't say anything, says Mona, who has just caught her breath. He didn't blink. He didn't scratch either himself or me. He didn't go to the bathroom. He didn't speak to Mary Smith or adjust her bonds. He didn't turn on the T.V. He didn't drink his water. He didn't bring me more water. He didn't check to make sure the stove was off. He didn't play music. He didn't sleep or stretch or yawn to indicate that he might wish to go to sleep soon. He didn't do anything. He just sat there all the rest of the night—which comprised several hours—gazing across the table over the brim of that stupid bowl, as if at me, but I don't think so, says Mona. And I just sat and looked at him too, because, for the life of me, I couldn't think of anything else to do. Hmmm, says Henry. And by the end of the night, says Mona, that is just as the sun was rising and traffic could be heard again from the street, we both had become terribly restless from sitting at that table so long without saying or doing anything. Here we are, says Henry.

Mona and Henry stand in front of a door that says 5— with the last two digits missing. Henry plunges his hand into his pocket for his keys.

We were both so restless, says Mona, that we both had to get up, which we did, and engage in some violent activity, which we did. And what was that? says Henry, pushing open the door and reaching in to flip on the light switch.

We scarfed down the contents of that metal bowl, says Mona, and then we kicked and beat Mary Smith. We did so for half an hour or until she stopped struggling. Then the guy went back to his table, and I walked back to the establishment without saying good bye.

So whaddaya think? says Henry gesturing widely at the interior of his hotel room which is exactly like any other all right hotel room except that it has been painted entirely white. That is the brown wood paneled walls have been painted white, the orange carpeted floor has been painted white, the dirty white stucco ceiling has been painted white, the black cabinet of the T.V. has been painted white, the small maroon fridge in back has been painted white, the wooden night stands on either side of the big double bed have been painted white, and even the many colored bedclothes on the big double bed and the big double bed itself have been painted white.

It smells like paint, says Mona. You get used to it, says Henry. Sure, says Mona. Make yourself at home, says Henry. I'll get some hooch out of the fridge.

I think this is an all right room, says Mona, seating herself gingerly on the painted bedclothes at the end of the bed. But the paint smell would really get to me after a while. It does, says Henry, joining her with a tall glass of hooch in either hand. Sometimes it really gets to me. Hey! You've got a T.V.! says Mona. That's all right! I never watch it, says Henry. It came with the room, but whenever I turn it on I can't make head or tails of what the little people are talking about.

That's real funny, Henry, says Mona, taking Henry's ears gently in her fingers and turning his head so she can look him in the face. It's just like that with me. I can watch the little people in the T.V. for hours on end, and never gain the faintest clue as to what's going on. It can get very frustrating. When you watch for a long time, and you still don't have the faintest clue, it can get intensely frustrating, can't it, Henry? Well, says Henry. I mean sometimes, says Mona, it's enough to drive me batty. What was it exactly, says Henry, gently removing Mona's fingers from his ears and pushing a glass of hooch into her hand, that you scarfed down from that large metal bowl covered with cheese cloth?

Mary Smith: I lay in a white smock on a floor of pounded earth. The wind pressed its soft face against the curtain. Someone was coming for me, but that same someone was not coming for me. Outside the immense white moon hung indifferently in the black and beyond its gradiated rings stars were only nicked into the unpredicated sky. Damp pushed up slowly through my vestments. Many colored smells rose, intermingled and locked. It was that lattice that I saw when I opened my eyes. Sand. The sheen of olives. Someone was coming but frozen in his progress. The moment unfolded into an infinite segmentation. Into that segmentation, I became lost. I became lost.

Mona slumps backwards onto the painted bed. Impossible to say, she says, gazing up at the stucco ceiling. We ate it so quickly, I hardly tasted it at all, and what I did taste was unrecognizable. Maybe it was a roast, says Henry. No, says Mona. A stew? says Henry. No, says Mona. Maybe a sausage of some kind? says Henry. Umm... no, says Mona. Perhaps a duck? says Henry. Don't think so, says Mona. A hen? says Henry. No, says Mona. A partridge? says Henry. No, says Mona. A grouse, pheasant or turkey? says Henry. No, says Mona. The thing we ate was roughly spherical in shape, and the insides were reminiscent of scrambled eggs, and if I'm not mistaken, it had eyes. A potato! says Henry. No, says Mona.

Well, says Henry. It sounds like an unusual dish. That is to say, rare. Though I've heard that in distant and obscure places, it is consumed more frequently than in the environs where you and I customarily find ourselves. Do you feel something, Mona? A lightness in the pit of the stomach, for example. It's the hooch, says Mona. I feel something, says Henry. Rare? says Mona. But not so rare, says Henry, in obscure and distant regions. But even in those places, never what you would call a staple. A little too rich. No. Not something upon which you'd sup, say, every morning. But not completely unheard of either—say Mona, says Henry, falling backwards to join Mona on the painted bedclothes. Is there something funny about this room? You wouldn't say it was spinning, for example.

It's the hooch, says Mona. Not completely unheard of? No, says Henry. Even I, on exceedingly rare, rare almost to the point of being imaginary, occasions have dealt in articles of the type you may have consumed in the frenzy that came upon you that strange morning after the long uneventful night you spent in the plant cluttered and newspaper strewn room of the guy from the hooch depot. You seem to really have the low down, says Mona, maybe you should take a look at this.

The bed clothes crackle as Mona sits up. She jerks her oversized furry purse into her lap, opens it, and begins digging around inside.

I've had this for a while, says Mona. A friend gave it to me. I've watched it over and over, but for the life of me, it doesn't make any sense. Here. Mona pulls a fairly large rectangular plastic box out of her purse and shoves it at Henry.

What is it? says Henry. I just told you I don't know, says Mona. I want you to figure it out. Well, where did you get it? says Henry. A guy gave it to me. He was a friend of mine, I think, says Mona. A friend? says Henry. I think, says Mona. It's hard to say. He gave it to you? says Henry. Yes, says Mona. Well, he didn't exactly give it to me. It was more like he left it somewhere where I was sure to find it and pick it up. I see, says Henry. No you don't, says Mona. Why don't we insert it into the machine under the T.V. and look at it? It's a video? says Henry. No duh, says Mona. I love videos, says Henry, and he grabs the rectangular box from Mona and quickly sticks it into the machine under the T.V. The machine hums and whirrs.

I've always wanted to deal in videos, says Henry, flicking on the T.V. whose screen blinks and flashes to life in the manner of a great gray eye opening. But I never have. No? says Mona. No, says Henry. It's always been my ambition to deal in videos but never my achievement. That's too bad, says Mona. Not at all, says Henry. Certain ambitions are meant to become achievements in short order. But others, such as dealing in videos, are meant to be continually and perpetually forestalled so as to always remain ambitions and never to be realized. I don't get you, says Mona. Shsh! says Henry. It's starting.

Mona and Henry turn their attention to the T. V. The image of a rat scuttles across the bottom of the otherwise empty screen. So it's about rats, is it? says Henry. Mona says nothing.

Nothing more happens in the T.V. for several minutes. Henry and Mona wait. Very suddenly, there is a landscape with a human figure in it. Hey! says Henry, I think I know that place. Shsh! says Mona.

Somewhere on the periphery of the enormous vacant lot behind the big building in which conventions are sometimes held, Jack lies supine in a shallow ditch. Suspended above him by a string, the sun, an oversized yellow pie plate upon which is emblazoned the face of Little Jack, grimaces down at him. Jack's eyes open. He remains silent, supine and unmoving for some time. Finally, he speaks.

Jack: Hey buddy!

(no response)

Jack (louder): Hey buddy!

(no response)

Hey! says Henry. That's that guy Jack who won the whistling contest at the convention I was telling about. I thought you said you didn't know him. Shsh, says Mona. There's someone else.

Jack (louder still): Hey buddy! Do you think it's safe here?

A voice: Oh yeah.

Jack: Are you sure?

The voice: Oooh yeah.

Jack props himself up on his elbow. He glances about his surroundings.

Jack: Are you positive?

The voice: Oooh yeah. Positive.

Jack: It's not safe inside.

The voice: Right.

Jack: On account of the nightmares.

The voice: Right.

Jack: Like the one I was just having.

The voice: Right. But you've forgotten it now, haven't you?

Jack: Funny!

The voice: Oh yeah.

Jack: It's funny.

The voice: Right.

Jack: It's funny. I hadn't forgotten it until just now when you told me I'd forgotten it. Even now I vividly remember remembering my nightmare, but the nightmare I remember remembering has escaped me completely.

The voice: Look Jack, nice psychological observations like the one you've recently served up, are not, if you catch my drift, of overwhelming interest to me.

Jack: Mona often told me that.

The voice: Chump!

At the mention of Mona, the sun jerks and twitches at the end of its string.

Hey! They're talking about you! says Henry. No, someone else, says Mona. A different "Mona."

Jack: Hey buddy!

The voice (fatigued): Oh god!

Jack (looking up, furtively, at the sun):   Are you sure it's safe here?

The voice: Why don't you leave me alone?

Jack: There's something funny about that sun.

The voice: You're hopeless, Jack.

Jack: And that too. How do you know my name is Jack?

The voice: I was speaking generically.

Jack: Still, it's quite a coincidence, isn't it?

The voice: Don't make anything of it.

Jack: I mean, your name isn't "buddy" is it?

The voice: Well... no.

Jack: But my name is actually "Jack." So when you were addressing me generically, you were also addressing me by name.

The voice: Big deal.

Jack: It's quite a coincidence.

The voice: Look, Jack. It's no coincidence. First off I was addressing you generically. Second off, everyone's name is actually "Jack."

Jack: Everyone's?

The voice: Everyone's.

Jack: What about Mary Smith, for example?

They're talking about Mary Smith now! says Henry. No, says Mona. That's a different "Mary Smith."

The voice: Her name's "Jack."

Jack: How about Parson Smith?

They're talking about Parson Smith now! says Henry. No, says Mona, that's a different "Parson Smith."

The voice: "Jack."

Jack: The guy at the hooch depot?

Hey, they're—says Henry. No, says Mona, it's a different "guy from the hooch depot."

Jack: But what about Mona? Surely her name isn't—

The voice: "Jack"

I think that that time he was talking about you, says Henry. No, says Mona, he wasn't. The first time he mentioned my name, he was talking about a different "Mona." And in this more recent instance, he was also talking about a different "Mona." It is possible that the second different "Mona" is distinct from the first different "Mona." But I can assure you that neither "Monas" refer to myself because I have never met this "Jack." Nor have I ever met any other

"Jack" hitherto mentioned by anyone. Though I have met a "Jack" but that was in very fleeting and unusual circumstances, and that "Jack" is notably distinct from all the others.

Jack: But what about you? What's your name?

The voice: Do you want to know how long I've been here?

Jack: Sure.

The voice: I can't tell you.

Jack: I see.

The voice: Shut up! "I see." I hate that. Shut up and listen! I can't tell you how long I've been here because I don't know. That is, now I don't know. I used to know. I even used to know how I got here.

Jack: I remember how I got here quite well. There was an unfortunate accident involving myself, two acquaintances of mine, some rats, and—

The voice: Yes, yes, yes. Of course, you do. At first I knew how I got here too. I remembered it in every detail. I remembered being someplace else. I remembered arriving here. And I remembered every sequential moment of the intervening time.

Jack: The journey is kind of a blur for me. But the events that led up to it are crystal clear. See, a long, long time ago, there was this little guy...

(A violent conflagration involving wind and thunder is heard coming from somewhere else. Jack's voice is swallowed up in the noise. The sun, upon which is emblazoned the face of Little Jack, begins to swing back and forth like a pendulum. After some time, the noise and wind subside, but the sun continues to swing. Jack is covered by a thin layer of gray dust.)

The voice (quietly): Would you please try to keep your mouth shut. I'm trying to help you. I'm trying to give you the "low down" so to speak.

The voice (confidentially): I remembered all that too. And I kept remembering it for some time. And in addition, I remembered the days that were accumulating here, featureless as they were.

Jack: Featureless. That's good news.

The voice: And I kept remembering those days for a long time. At least, how many there were. But then something happened.

Jack: Featureless days are O.K. by me. I have lived many a featureless day and hope to live many more. Before I came here during the long days in my comfortable though frequently empty domicile, often in the lulling moments that took place just at the peak of the afternoon, when it was revealed that not a damn thing was going to happen that day, I always reminded myself that a featureless day of viscid, white, paste-like time was a thing to be cherished and enjoyed.   Especially when you consider the alternatives.

(A ne'er-do-well pokes his head and torso over the crest of the ridge of dirt behind Jack. His face is torn and broken. The eyes of the face have been burnt out of it, leaving two large black craters. Jack starts at the noise of dirt moving, turns to face the ne'er-do-well and is horrified.)

Jack: Whoa buddy!

The voice (emitted from the mouth of the ne'er-do-well): I don't know what happened. But shortly after it did, I instantly forgot all the events previous to my arrival, how I had arrived and the number of days I had been here.

Jack: Whoa! Buddy!

The voice: You'd think that would have been very disorienting, wouldn't you?   But it wasn't. It had exactly the opposite effect. In fact, I've never felt so oriented in my life.

Jack: But what happened to your face?

The voice: What?

Jack: Forget it.

The voice: Shut the hell up.

Jack: What's that?

(Jack points to a ridge of dirt some distance to his right where an exceptionally large rat has appeared. The rat rears up on its hind legs so that its soft belly and whiskered snout are silhouetted against the pale yellow sky.)

It *is* about rats, says Henry. Shsh! says Mona. There's more.

The rat: Don't be glum, chums! Don't be sad! Soon   at   a   certain   establishment,   a   grand entertainment's to be had!

(The rat drops on all fours and disappears behind the ridge of dirt.)

Jack:

The voice:

Jack:

The voice:

Jack: Was it speaking in rhyme?

(The rat re-emerges on the lip of dirt. It is now clad in a rat-sized pink and white tutu in which get up it begins to cut capers and cavort along the top of the ridge.)

The rat: There'll be singing!   There'll be dancing! There'll be magic and romancing!   Come one! Come all!   For a free forgetting and a fall!

(The rat scuttles away.   Its bare tail trails snake-like in the dirt behind it, surrounded by its hindquarters, which are haloed by the pink and white tutu.)

Jack:

The voice:

Jack: I'll remember that.

The voice: Chump!

(Jack rolls onto his back and watches the sun swing back and forth above him.)

Jack (sighing): Oh boy.

The voice: Right.

Jack: I sure wish Mona were here.   If she were here, I'm sure she'd say something plucky at this point.

I'm sure she'd say something plucky and full of fresh initiative. If Mona were here, she'd probably say: Let's get out of this dump and go find some hooch somewhere.

Are you sure he's not referring to you? says Henry. Yes, says Mona. That sure sounded like you, says Henry.

Are you incapable, says Mona, of grasping the possibility that somewhere out in the wide world there exists a woman possessing many, or perhaps all, of the characteristics you would attribute to me and whose name is "Mona" but who remains clearly and irrevocably distinct from myself?

Well, says Henry.

Jack: Hey Buddy! I think I'm going to have to leave shortly. I'm going to look for some hooch, just like Mona would if she were here. You're welcome to accompany me. Maybe we can find that certain establishment the rat spoke of.

The voice: Chump!

Jack (rising): Suit yourself.

(The figure of a ne'er-do-well can be seen rising behind Jack. It gropes forward over the uneven ground until it bumps into Jack.)

(The ne'er-do-well catches hold of Jack's belt with one hand, which upon close inspection looks more like a claw. Jack bolts across the broken field, dragging the ne'er-do-well behind. The sun, which has descended to eye level, pursues. One after the other, each of these figures reaches the border of the screen, takes a short hop, as if over a puddle, and disappears. The screen goes black.)

Who did you say gave it to you? says Henry, extracting the video from the machine. Some guy, says Mona. It wouldn't have been the "Jack" you met under fleeting and unusual circumstances, would it? says Henry. No, says Mona. A completely different guy.

At this point, I would suggest, says Henry, that it might have been me if I hadn't already told you that I'd never dealt in videos. That's too bad, says Mona, if you had suggested that it was you who had given me the video—or rather left it someplace where I was sure to pick it up—as an anonymous token say of love or friendship—I would have believed you. Really? says Henry. Yes, says Mona, and believing you, I would have felt a shock of recognition and a great shifting inside, as my mind, having been thrown seining back into the dark ocean of my memory, netted and in that way saved, your face there among the coral of anonymous ne'er-do-well faces.

I would have liked it if I had said that and you had believed me, says Henry. It is not often that I'm believed even when I'm telling the God's honest truth. I know what you mean, says Mona. And I'm impressed that you, even having been repeatedly chastened in the fires of disbelief, have, throughout my entire discourse, which I confess has been prolonged and at points whimsical, to say the least, maintained an admirably credulous posture. Thank you, says Henry. And you have lovely ears with which you listen, says Mona, putting her fingers again on Henry's ears. Thanks, says Henry. They're like haikus stuck to either side of your head, says Mona.

You mentioned another video? says Henry, gently removing Mona's fingers from his ears. Oh yeah, says Mona. Just a minute. And she digs once more in her oversized furry purse, and once again pulls from it, a black plastic box which Henry quickly inserts into the machine under the television set. The machine hums and whirrs. Henry and Mona are silent. The gray eye opens on a landscape viewed from a tremendous height.

The landscape is mostly empty, but there is a small square structure near the left hand corner of the screen. It looks like a sugar cube. Along part of one edge of this structure, there extrudes a tessellated incline. It is along this incline that two specks are inching upwards. Their progress might be compared to that of two very small insects, fleas for example, scaling, in infinitesimal hops and leaps, a short curb at the edge of a narrow street in one of the more insignificant neighborhoods of a nondescript town. There is the sound of two men panting close by. A small gold arrow is illuminated, pointing at one of the specks. Jack's voice breaks in.

Jack's voice: Wow! This is an exceedingly long journey we find ourselves on.

That's Jack's voice! says Henry. You think so? says Mona. I'm virtually sure of it, says Henry. And it's my guess that that arrow there is intended to indicate that that speck over there on the left is the one currently speaking, in this case, Jack. Hmm..., says Mona. Oh look! says Henry, The other arrow is lighting up!

The voice's voice: Long, long, long...

-an arrow—

Jack's voice: Uncannily long.

-an arrow—

The voice's voice: Long, long, long...

-an arrow—

Jack's voice: Illogically long.

-an arrow—

The voice's voice: Long, long, long...how so?

-an arrow—

Jack's voice: I've passed this way before.

-an arrow—

The voice's voice: Chump!

-an arrow—

Jack's voice: It was on my way out to the huge lot with the ditches from which we are now returning.

-an arrow—

The voice's voice: Right, right, long, long...

-an arrow—

Jack's voice: I tell you I passed by this way on my earlier journey to the place from which we are returning right now.

-an arrow—

The voice's voice: And?

-an arrow—

Jack's voice: It was shorter.

-an arrow—

The voice's voice:

-an arrow—

Jack's voice: It should have been longer. It should have been longer by exactly as much distance as stretches from my domicile to where we are right now. According to geometry, a constituent line segment cannot be longer than the segment that contains it.

-an arrow—

The voice's voice: Oh God!

-an arrow—

Jack: I learned that in school, and I still remember it.

-an arrow—

The voice: Take a look at this!

The gray eye blinks.

Jack and the figure of the broken faced ne'er-do-well from which the voice has emitted can be seen silhouetted against the yellow sky, standing at the top of the stairs in front of the big building in which conventions are sometimes held. The steps stretch infinitely downwards below them. They are panting heavily. Simultaneously, they both collapse in the shade under a concrete awning that hangs above a pair of big double doors.

See, says Henry. It was Jack. Huh? says Mona. The voice we heard before was coming from the speck on the left as the arrow indicated, and now we can see that that speck was Jack. Jack? says Mona. The guy who won the whistling contest, says Henry. The one you met under fleeting and unusual circumstances. The one who may have left the video tape we are now watching someplace where you were sure to stumble over it and pick it up! No, says Mona. All of those were different "Jacks."

(The broken faced ne'er-do-well stands up, sticks one claw-like hand into his back pocket, and pulls out a worn leather wallet. He drops the wallet in front of Jack, then stuffs as much of the claw-like hand as will fit into his own mouth, and begins hopping about in a state of great agitation. Jack, oblivious to the agitation of the other, unfolds the wallet, inserts his fingers along its inner edges, pulls it open and turns it upside down. Several dog-eared cards, some rotting money and a few worn slips of paper flutter to the ground. Jack scoops up the money.)

Jack: Hey! We can get some hooch with this!

(The ne'er-do-well, hopping more manically, pushes the remaining cards and slips of paper towards Jack with his foot, which has come out its shoe and has only three horny toes.)

The voice: Mumph! Mum mumph!

Jack (picking up a card an examining it): Hmm...

The voice: Mummumph! Mummumph!

Jack: Good God!

The voice: Mummumph! Mummumph!

Jack: According to this...

The voice: Mummummummummummumph!

Jack (leaping to his feet): Dad!

Jack's father: Jack!

(They embrace. Jack looks into the broken visage of the ne'er-do-well from which the voice has been emitted. Jack's father looks into Jack's face. After a time, Jack slumps to the ground.)

Jack's father: I -

Jack: Yes?

Jack's father: No.

Jack: Oh.

Jack's father: There's something-

Jack: Yes?

Jack's father: No.

Jack: Oh.

Jack's father: O.K.

Jack: Yes?

(Jack's father rises and assumes a posture of declamation. He clears his throat. He clears his throat again. He runs one claw-like hand through his hair. Oddly, a feather is discharged with this motion.)

Jack's father: Now listen close young son. What I have to tell you is very important and I have a strong intuition that I will not have the opportunity to repeat it.

Jack: C'mon dad.

Jack's father: I'm not kidding, son. The world's a larger and more sinister place than you can possibly have imagined. There are inscrutable and unscrupulous forces at work in it. While those forces are usually utterly indifferent to the comings and goings of the likes of you and I, I have a very strong intuition that they would go great lengths to prevent me from disclosing to you what I'm about to disclose.

Jack: Geeze, dad. It's been such a long time since I've seen you, and now here you are and—

Jack's father: Hush! Time's awasting!

Jack: I mean I confess for a long time remembering you was not an activity which I voluntarily engaged in, but now, here beside the glass doors to the big building in which conventions are sometimes held, with the hostile sun floating out there barely at bay-

Jack's father: Be still! This no time for cheap sentimentality! Now listen close: Not too long ago, I found myself hanging around the neighborhood looking for free hooch as I was wont to do in those days, and the weather was especially congenial. You might say, unnaturally congenial. Are you listening, son?

Jack: I feel a slight but growing blush of filial affection pushing up through the sludge of my long resentment not unlike a weed or prairie flower might push up through hair-like fissures in a slab of concrete or granite under which—

Jack's father: It was like a vision, son! It was like a dream! The sunlight winked and sparkled on the sidewalks, and Morning, fresh as a twelve year old virgin garlanded with daisies, skipped and gamboled across the dew kissed lawns.

Jack: —it was deposited as a seed.

Jack's father: And I felt fine, my boy. I felt terrific. I felt like something was sure to happen that day, something big and consequential.

Jack: I've often felt that way, dad. But nothing's ever come of it.

Jack's father: But this time something did, my boy. As I was slouching around the sidewalk, whistling in spite of my hang-over, I came across two children who were uncannily clean and virtually indistinguishable from each other. The first child said: We have often seen you coming and going, and we have wondered why, in your comings and goings, you have never stopped up to visit us. And I said, Where do you live? And the second child said, We'll show you. And so they did. They led me to a squat residential building nearby, and up through its untidy vestibule and staircase to a little room on the third floor.

Jack: I've heard of that room.

Jack's father: But there was nothing in that room! It was empty. Just a stained orange carpet and a lot of dust. That was all. Or so I thought when I first went in. 'Cuz then the first child disappeared into the kitchen, and when he came back he had something in his hands. The something was wriggling and making small shrieking noises. The wriggling and shrieking thing was a rat. It was wriggling and shrieking because it was encased in an apparatus which pierced its wriggling body at several junctures. This apparatus was ingenious and extremely uncomfortable and it was within this apparatus that the rat twisted and suffered.

So it *is* about rats, says Henry. No, says Mona, there's more.

A line of red lettering flashes across the bottom of the screen. It reads:

During the course of the following speech by Jack, Jack's father will undergo a strange transformation. His arms will shrink into his sleeves and fold up close against his body. His body will grow out of his clothes and become covered with feathers. His mouth and nose will converge into a beak. Near the end of this elaborate and uncomfortable process—which will coincide with the end of Jack's speech—Jack's father will begin pecking at the concrete.

The camera zooms in on Jack's face until only his lips, his teeth, his tongue and his uvula are visible. These organs shake and move together as he speaks.

Jack's mouth: That's horrifying, and it confirms the rather low opinion I have always held of those children. Not that I sympathize with rats mind you. Vile, disgusting creatures in my book. Except perhaps the one I saw earlier cavorting about in a pink and white tutu. That was something altogether different. Hey! Maybe we should head out to the establishment it spoke of. Even though I've never been there, not even in disguise, I feel sure there'll be hooch available, and I tell ya, I could really use some. Whaddaya say, Dad?

—Jack's mouth closes—

Jack's father's voice can be heard from off screen.

Jack's father's voice: Not... much... time.

—Jack's mouth opens.—

Jack's mouth: Dad?

Jack's father's voice: The rat... as... it... twisted and... suffered... told me... secret... the secret... was...

Jack's mouth: Are you O.K. ?

The noises of scratching and pecking.

Jack's mouth:

The screen goes blank.

Well? says Mona. Yes? says Henry. Well? says
Mona. Yes? says Henry. Well, what do you make
of them? says Mona. Ahh, says Henry. Make of
them, yes. The videotapes, says Mona. What do
you make of the two videotapes we have seen so
far? Right, right, says Henry. The videotapes.
What do I make of them. Yes, says Mona. Right,
says Henry. Well? says Mona. Yes? says Henry.
Go ahead, says Mona. Huh? says Henry. I'm
becoming frustrated, says Mona. I'm sorry, says
Henry. Well then? says Mona. Ye-, says Henry.
Shut up! says Mona, and she grabs hold of Henry's
head by his delicate ears and turns it toward herself.
Then she brings her face very close to Henry's as if
she were trying to speak to a dog.

I am asking you, says Mona, to make interpretive
comments on the two videotapes we have viewed
so far. It is my hope that the comments you're
going to make will prove insightful and illuminating
as I myself haven't been able to make head or tail of
the videotapes, and this incapacity disturbs me
somewhat. If you think back a little bit, perhaps

you will recall that such was my precisely stated purpose in showing you these videotapes in the first place. Right, right, says Henry. I get you. You can let go of my ears now. Henry gently disengages Mona's fingers from his ears. Well? says Mona.

It's like this, says Henry. These videotapes are about the problems your friend "Jack"—It's a different "Jack" says Mona. A different "Jack, " says Henry. It's all about the problems he has had with rodents of a certain rat-like variety. Ah ha, says Mona, go on. O.K., says Henry. Now just suppose, this "Jack" some time ago, had holed himself up in a room. Say a hotel room, for example. Say one just like this one, for example. Say one just like this one to the degree that everything inside it had been painted white, for example. Ahh... O.K., says Mona.

He had holed himself up in a room just like this one, says Henry, to get away from it all, as they say. That is he had sought out on purpose a relatively neutral space, which was as phenomenally empty—that is to say, void, void of phenomena—as possible. To get away from it all. To escape, for a time, from the hurly-burly of the rough and tumble world.

What? says Mona. Out there, says Henry.

He was here? says Mona.

No, says Henry. He had holed himself up in a room very much like this one, but not this one, in an attempt to escape a rough and tumble world very much like the one beyond that door, but not the same as the one beyond that door.

He was here? says Mona.

No, says Henry. I am speaking analogically. What? says Mona. In my analogy, says Henry, there is a room belonging to "Jack," whoever he might be, that corresponds to this room in every detail. Hence the door to that room corresponds to the door in this room—that is to say, that door—Henry points at the door. Furthermore, then, the rough and tumble world beyond the door to Jack's room according to my analogy, corresponds, roughly, to the rough and tumble world out there, says Henry, jabbing at the door vigorously.

So he wanted to get away from it all, says Mona. Exactly, says Henry. That is to say all of it. That is to say everything. Henry nods. O.K. I'm with you, says Mona. Go on. And so he did, says Henry, and everything was fine. Well, that's nice, says Mona.

That is, says Henry, taking a healthy belt from the bottle, it was fine for a while. For a couple of days maybe, or a couple of months, or it might have been that things were fine only for a couple of hours, or only for the first hour. That is possible too, says Henry. But soon enough—this is where the rats come in—one night while he was laying sleepless on top of the painted bed clothes, he started hearing noises. The rats, says Mona. Right, says Henry. They were scratching noises of the kind frequently made by rodents of the rat-like variety. And while at first these noises were furtive and intermittent, in the course of a few days—or possibly hours, or possibly one hour—they grew to be deafening and relentless. What a shitty room that guy got, says Mona. No kidding, says Henry, and what with those deafening and relentless rat noises pouring into his ears hour after hour, day after day, perhaps month after month, coming as they were from the walls of the very room to which he had come seeking sanctuary from precisely that kind of thing... He just lost it. He went rocketing right out of his senses. Started jabbering to himself, chuckling out of context, drooling etc... until he finally ran raving into the streets, ended up in a ditch, met a voice that was emitted from the broken face of a ne'er-do-well, saw a rat in a tutu, climbed a very long staircase, found out that the voice was really his very own father, listened to a bullshit story about a couple of children, and watched his father turn into a big chicken. And that's that! says Henry. Whaddaya think?

I think what I've thought all along but have chosen not to reveal to you, says Mona, clenching Henry's ears again between her strong fingers, but this time with such force that it is unlikely that he will be able to remove them.

I think everyone on the videotapes, says Mona, the voice, Jack and the rats most of all, were lying to me. And I think you too, Henry, have been lying to me. And I think everyone I've ever met has always lied to me. And I think I, for one, in fact the only one, have always told the truth even when it didn't make any sense to me. And I think, more than anything, that this whole situation is completely unfair.

The rats: At this point the tape becomes too garbled for us to conduct any further analysis. There is the sound of a struggle, a scream—we believe emitted from the throat of "Henry" but the lab has yet to make a conclusive identification—the sound of a door opening and closing, and several hours of soft plaintive moans—again we believe from "Henry" but positive identification has eluded us. What we have though is, we believe, more than enough to confirm our fondest hopes vis-à-vis the effectiveness of the efforts of our fine agents in disinformation and counter-propaganda. These efforts have successfully rendered the enemy thoroughly befuddled if not deluded. We can congratulate ourselves then that everything is proceeding smoothly, and, as the enemy appears to have no clue as to the true nature of the situation, we can expect with a high degree of confidence that the operation will soon succeed without the hindrance of counter-measures. Much will fall that day. So, go smilingly about your work gentlemen, and always remember, "We take what falls."

Mona pads down the last flight of stairs and into the courtyard in the back of the nondescript hotel, swabbing triangles of blood from the corners of her mouth with the end of her tongue.

It is dawn, and a pink sheet of dawn light is settling itself gently over the broken surface of the jade water in the swimming pool. Under the water, near the center of the pool, the body of Mary Smith floats among the folds of her white nighty.

Mona crosses the patio and stretches out on her belly across the concrete apron, with her head hanging over the water.

mary smith: Mona?

Propping herself up on her elbow, Mona examines her own reflection drawn crazily on the pool's surface, clears her throat and hawks a clam sized yellow loogie into the water. The surface of the water spasms into flocks of ripples.

Don't spit in the pool, girlie.

An old man in a white bathrobe stands behind Mona. He's holding a white plastic ice bucket against his hip.

There are those of us who like to swim there, says the old man. There are those of us who like to rise before the street lights come on, and slip our pale, sleep-sick bodies into the water before it loses its chill.

Sorry, baby, says Mona.

You're not sorry, says the old man.

He walks to the edge of the pool, sets down the white plastic ice bucket and shrugs his robe from his shoulders. His body is skinny and furry with big patches of wiry white hair and smaller streaks of softer black hair. His business hangs limply between his legs like a clump of mushrooms.

Is that dead girl a friend of yours? says the old man, pointing at the body of Mary Smith, which remains suspended near the center of the pool among the swirls of her white nighty.

What? says Mona.

The old man slides into the pool and begins to swim with long slow strokes in a wide circle close to the edge.

This town is the pits, says Mona. I used to reside in another town. It was completely different. It was more congenial, for example. Also there was more hooch, and the hooch was more readily available.

The old man hauls himself out of the water near Mona and stands up. His wiry hair is pressed against his body and curled around his business.

I know that town, says the old man. I built that town with my own two hands. I'm a magnate.

Big deal, says Mona.

You say that because you don't know what a magnate is, says the magnate.

I can see what's standing here dripping right in front of me, says Mona.

Sure you can, says the magnate.

The sun has climbed into morning. Long shadows fall into the courtyard and around the pool in confused patterns. Someone opens a door on one of the upper floors of the hotel.

Why don't you take me back to that other town, says Mona. I've always wanted to go back, but I never have because I can never remember exactly where it is.

Someone on one of the upper floors of the hotel screams in agony.

The magnate pulls his lips back over his teeth and makes a strained wheezing, laughing noise. Then he hunches over so his head is hanging just above his business. Then he straightens up. A ropy strand of saliva stretches from his shoulder to the corner of his mouth.

Are you all right? says Mona.

I'm going back to my room, says the magnate. Then I'm going to fill this bucket with ice. Then I'm coming back here. If you're here when I get back, I'll take you to that town I built.

I'll be here, says Mona.

The magnate grabs his robe and throws it over one shoulder. He pads across the patio to the stairs. His buttocks are hairy and bony. Mona looks at the water in the pool, which is no longer pink but more greenish.

Traffic grinds into motion on the street. A T.V. is turned on somewhere.

Mona sucks her teeth and watches the water in the pool.

The magnate returns wearing an orange leisure suit. Mona rises and takes his arm. They leave the hotel. They get into the magnate's car. They drive away.

The morning is bright and clean among the buildings.

Did you know that guy Henry who lived in the same hotel as you? says Mona. He sold me a chair once, says the magnate. Wicker? says Mona. Rattan, says the magnate. The whole world sucks if you ask me, says Mona.

They drive.

When we get to this town that we're going to, says the magnate, are you going to want me to tie you up? No, says Mona. In fact, I would prefer that you give me the widest possible leeway. That's good, says the magnate. I've never liked tying people up even when I've done it as a result of an irresistible compulsion. Compulsion? says Mona. I am on occasion seized with irresistible compulsions, says the magnate. And when that happens, all bets are off. I know what you mean, says Mona.

The city drops away behind them as the car ascends along the crease of a rounded hill covered with brown grass. Sporadically along the side of the road, large and medium-sized trees covered with orange leaves loom and dwindle, wildly. Sunlight tricks over the tops of the hills, and behind the hills, the mountains. The mountains are gray.

The town we are going to, says Mona, would you say it is more of a rural place than the town we just left? Rural, hmm... says the magnate. I was much younger when I lived there, says Mona. My recollection of the details is kind of hazy. Would you say, even in the brief time you knew him—when he was selling you that chair—that that fellow, Henry, was he a friend of yours? I wanted a wicker chair, says the magnate. What I got was rattan. I put it in the trunk. The whole world sucks, says Mona, and yet the scenery, here on this road, is O.K.

The car pulls off the paved road upon which they have been traveling, and onto a dirt road that ascends more sharply into the mountains. The trees look like explosions.

Building that town, says the magnate, was the result of an irresistible compulsion. I was very able bodied back then. I could take things apart and I could put them together, and I could engage in either activity for long hours over the course of several months without sleeping or eating or desisting in any way. But the most amazing thing about it, was this dog. Dog? says Mona.

This dog used to hang around one of the construction sites, says the magnate. A relatively insignificant one. The site was on the periphery of the town then under construction which of course meant that as the town grew, this particular site became more and more peripheral as it was shifted further and further from the center. The dog who used to hang out at that site became more and more peripheral as well and would have dwindled to an insignificance bordering on non-existence were it not able to talk which is extraordinary and noteworthy for a dog no matter where it hangs out. I saw a talking dog in a show once, says Mona. The show was at a certain establishment where I used to work occasionally. That was a trick, says the magnate. A stoolie crouched behind the dog and talked for it. The dog was chewing peanut butter. You would have noticed if you had been watching closely.

Darkness falls onto the road through the exploding forest on the side of the gray mountain up which they are traveling. The magnate turns the headlights on. The road washes gray. The trees turn black.

The dog I am speaking of, says the magnate, spoke without the assistance of stoolies of any kind. It didn't chew peanut butter. It chewed tobacco. I saw a monkey chew tobacco once, says Mona. But it wasn't part of a show. The monkey chewed tobacco backstage between acts. That's just how it was with this dog, says the magnate. He didn't chew tobacco as part of a performance. He chewed tobacco because it was one of his habits. This was also exactly the case with his talking. The monkey I met didn't talk at all, says Mona. Still I liked it. I liked also that it didn't talk. Of course it did have other disgusting habits more common to monkeys.

This dog was an exemplary animal in all his habits, says the magnate. His name was Ralph.

The car passes between two street lights, which are on, and onto a paved street with short buildings. No one seems to be around. The car glides alone over conical shadows on the pavement.

Is this the town you built and I came from? says Mona. The very same, says the magnate. Where are all the people? says Mona. It may be quieter than you remember it, says the magnate. It may be much quieter than you remember it. It's a big town all right. It goes on for miles and miles, and what you said about its congeniality and the availability of hooch are still true today. But it has gotten quieter in recent times, much quieter.

The magnate stops the car and rolls down his window. Wind comes into the car. The trees, which are still out there somewhere beyond the town they have just entered, rustle.

Mona can't bring herself to say anything.

The magnate rolls the window back up and shifts the car back into gear. The car cruises past the end of a block and starts down a new one.

That Ralph was some dog, says the magnate. And boy what a talker!

Do you remember that man you saw me with last night? says Mona. The same one who sold you the wicker chair that was really rattan?

Ralph even told jokes, says the magnate.

What was that guy's name? says Mona. I can't quite remember what his name was.

The car turns a corner.

The jokes Ralph told, says the magnate, were often so oblique that no-one could get them. But I always laughed anyway because I liked Ralph. In the end, we had to put him to sleep.

Where are we? says Mona.

The car has pulled up in front of a squat nondescript building with a garish green neon sign over the door. The door is open, and the room inside throws a carpet of yellow light out across the wide sidewalk. A very large woman in a yellow house dress has settled her bulk into one of two pink and green lawn recliners beside the door.

Let's get out now, says the magnate.

The stars, scattered across the sky like sequins across a black leotard, shake and flash. Far below them, crowds of loitering breezes mull through the empty streets of the town the magnate built and Mona

148

came from. On the outskirts of that town, dogs howl and moan.

Mary Smith? says Mona to the large woman in the yellow house dress.

No, says the woman.

Really? says Mona.

Really, says the woman.

I thought you were, says Mona, on account of your dress and the color of your recliner. Isn't that funny?

Not really, says the woman. Have a seat.

Mona sits down.

Here's the hooch! says the magnate, emerging from the squat building with a bottle and three glasses in his hands. You're the guy, says Mona. The magnate hands round the glasses and pours hooch into them. The hooch looks green in the neon light as do the faces of Mona, the magnate and the large woman. They all bend simultaneously to sip.

Great stuff! says the magnate. Sure, says the woman. Mona spits her hooch on the ground. This isn't hooch! says Mona. I don't know what it is, but it isn't hooch.   My mistake, says the magnate, gathering their glasses. I'll be right back.

I used to live in this town, says Mona to the large woman.

Really? says the woman.

I think so, says Mona. It was a long time ago and my memory isn't what it once was.

Right, says the woman.

Did you live here then? says Mona.

I don't think so, says the woman.

If you had lived here then, says Mona. You might have met me. We might have had a conversation or possibly an altercation or we might have conducted business together.

I don't think so, says the woman.

What happened to the old guy? says Mona.

The woman shrugs her shoulders.

Here's the hooch! says the magnate, returning with a new bottle and glasses. He passes the glasses around and pours hooch into them. You're the guy, says Mona. They all sip.

Great stuff! says the magnate. Sure, says the woman. Mona spits her hooch on the ground. That is not hooch, says Mona. I know hooch when I taste it, and that's not it. My mistake, says the magnate, gathering their glasses. The magnate overturns Mona's glass to pour the remainder of hooch onto the ground. I'll be right back.

I was really looking forward to getting here, says Mona to the woman. But now I feel a little disappointed.

Really? says the woman.

Yes, says Mona. In fact I find myself growing restless. It's possible that this restlessness will reach a degree of intensity that demands that I engage in some sort of violent activity.

Really? says the woman.

Yes, says Mona. I don't think you'll want to be around at that point. Although I can't remember any specific incident, I feel a strong intuition that when my restlessness reaches a certain degree of intensity, all bets are off, if you know what I mean.

The woman shrugs her shoulders.

Here's the hooch! says the magnate, emerging once again from the squat building. This time, he is carrying a bottle, three glasses and a jar of peanut butter.

Everything has taken on a dull olive coloring.

The magnate hands around the glasses and pours hooch into them. He sits on the ground and opens the jar of peanut butter. You're the guy, says Mona. They all sip.

Great stuff! says the magnate. Sure, says the woman. Mona spits her hooch on the ground. That tastes like rat poison! says Mona. Here's Ralph! says the magnate.

Ralph, says the woman.

I thought you put him to sleep, says Mona. I lied, says the magnate.

Ralph, the dog, trots into the pool of green light under the sign above the doorway of the nondescript building and sits on his haunches next to the magnate.

Watch this! says the magnate.

The magnate scoops out a rather large dollop of peanut butter with two of his fingers. Then he sticks those fingers in his mouth.

Hmmm... mmm... , says the magnate.

Ralph rears up on his hind legs and balances himself in that posture. He begins to declaim, gesturing as he speaks with his forepaws, which are as black as charcoal. Everything else is green.

Henry: I am mutilated, confused and unhappy. I never should have left my room. That is to say, I shouldn't have left my room to go to the establishment where I met the woman who calls herself "Mona." If I hadn't left my room on that occasion—and the innumerable other occasions I have neglected to mention—I do not believe I would be mutilated, confused and unhappy now; or at least, not as mutilated, confused and unhappy as I presently am. There is an object lesson in all this, and that lesson is: Never leave the room. It's not for me to be about wandering hither and yon with my eavesdropping ear and my voyeuristic eye. It's not for me to embark and listen and see with nothing but restlessness as my guide and counselor. It is for me to stay in my room even if it is completely inadequate to the purposes for which I acquired it. Even if, due to that inadequacy, staying in it amounts to a complete loss or failure. For this loss or failure, as complete and completely devastating as it will undoubtedly be, will be less complete and less completely devastating as the loss or failure that will follow from leaving which, as I stay, I know I will find myself wanting to do—as day melts into day and my restlessness grows and heaps and swells to unendurable intensities and as errant breezes throw open the door again and again to beckon with the long fingers of the spacious night. I will want to leave. But I will not. I will stay. I will continue rifling through this over-sized furry purse regardless of any and all exterior distractions. I will stay.

Oh boy! says Parson Smith to the bony, horse-faced girl behind the bar. It's good to get out of the house, and you really can't beat the hooch! The hooch here is terrible, says the girl, pushing a card Parson Smith has given her into her spangled brassiere. In fact, it is adulterated.

Ho! Ho! says Parson Smith. I'm not kidding, says the girl. I've adulterated it myself. Huh? says Parson Smith. There is a large plastic jug of hooch colored liquid in the basement, says the girl. Every morning, I go down there and bring that container up here and pour a measure of hooch-colored liquid into each of the bottles of hooch you see displayed on the shelves behind me. The measure I pour is usually equal to the amount of hooch that has been consumed the previous evening. I see, says Parson Smith. No you don't, says the girl. Even I don't know exactly what constitutes the hooch-colored liquid with which I adulterate the hooch we dispense to our customers. It could be, precisely, anything.

It's a nasty business, says Parson Smith. It sure is, says the horse-faced girl. And you don't know the half of it.

Tell it like it is, sister, mumbles a ne'er-do-well slumped over the bar with his head buried in his arms.

I want you both to know, says the girl refilling both the ne'er-do-well's and Parson Smith's glasses, that privately, I would never even consider participating in the questionable practices commonplace to an establishment such as this. But as an employee, I am constrained by the scruples, or unscrupulousness as is the case here, of my employer. I am, in essence, unfree. Ain't we all, says the ne'er-do-well. I suffer from a similar incapacity, says Parson Smith, and therefore sympathize. Parson Smith drains off the last of his hooch in one swig. But adulterated or not, says Parson Smith. This is fine hooch!

Hey! You're all right! says the horse-faced girl. My name's Sherry.

Sherry extends one long and bony-fingered hand to Parson Smith. Parson Smith, says Parson Smith, taking Sherry's hand into his own for a moment.

I don't want you to think less of the camaraderie we are now experiencing, says Parson Smith. But I feel constrained to tell you that under normal circumstances, I would be inclined to shun establishments of this sort, preferring instead the comforts and amenities of my own humble but cozy domicile. But due to the therapeutic aftermath of an unfortunate and, I am sure, misunderstood incident involving myself, my own better half, a former acquaintance of ours and a small child, that domestic refuge has become unavailable to me. In fact I find myself in a state of self-imposed exile, so to speak.

I hear you brother! says the ne'er-do-well.

Fortunately, says Parson Smith to the ne'er-do-well, this exile as painful and discomfiting as it is, has been ameliorated to a certain extent by my recent acquisition of a card, which I have given to yonder bartendress, which entitles me to all the hooch I can consume free from the necessity of remittance. Free hooch, says the ne'er-do-well. Lucky you.

Perhaps, says Parson Smith, you would be interested in hearing how I came to acquire that card? Sure, says Sherry. Not really, says the ne'er-do-well. It happened like this, says Parson Smith.

I was sitting on the curb in front of the above mentioned domicile, says Parson Smith, minding my own business which, I confess, at that moment amounted to little more than wallowing in self-pity, when without warning and without my having summoned it in anyway, a cab pulled up to the curb directly in front of me and stopped. The dirty window on the passenger's side inched down in jerks and starts, and the face, enormous nose first, of a certain cabby whom I vaguely recollected, emerged. Parson Smith? said the cabby. What? I said. Get in the cab, he said. What? I said again. I have a prize for you, he said. It's absolutely free.

Now I confess upon hearing the word "prize" and "absolutely free" I grew just a bit suspicious if not canny. In my experience, it hasn't been at all uncommon for the word "prize" to be used in such a fashion that it really denotes "onerous burden" and "absolutely free" has not infrequently been used so as to be synonymous with "at tremendous cost."

So in my canniness, says Parson Smith, I quickly devised a stratagem for dealing with this semi-stranger bearing tidings that appeared to be good, but might actually be quite bad. I decided to adopt a course of complete frankness. For, in my experience, often the best way to remain completely hidden from, and thus at an advantage to, a potential adversary has been to reveal everything and anything one has to hide in the frankest manner possible. Frankest? says Sherry. Frank what? says the ne'er-do-well. Frankest manner possible, says Parson Smith.

Whereas, I have also found, says Parson Smith, that it is it not at all uncommon for a posture of the utmost inscrutability to result in the disclosure of considerably more than one would like to disclose.

So, says Parson Smith, to this semi-stranger with his prominent if not menacing facial appendage and baldly stated but nonetheless ambiguous tidings, I spilled my guts as they say.

Now don't think I've been waiting here for you, I said. Under normal circumstances I wouldn't even be here on the curb for you to find, but rather tucked safely away in my snug domicile yonder, engaged in civic-minded projects of my own devising. But due to the therapeutic aftermath of an unfortunate incident, which has resulted in the prolonged absence if not irrevocable loss of my better half, that domestic refuge has been rendered unavailable to me. Indeed the prolonged absence, or possibly irrevocable loss, of my better half has shattered my sense of domestic security and overall well being, transforming the cozy domicile yonder into the dreariest of prisons.

Your better half wouldn't be Mary Smith, would she? said the cabby. You know her? I said. She's quite a number, ain't she? said the cabby. You know where she is? I said. Not the slightest clue, said the cabby. The prize I've got for you is a different kind of prize, and it's strictly on the up and up.

See, said the cabby, sometime ago a certain benefactor of yours, who may in fact have been you yourself, wrote your name on a slip of paper, put that slip of paper into an envelope and mailed that envelope to a large organization. This organization also received countless other envelopes with countless other slips of paper with countless other addresses and names. The organization employed its minions in opening each and every envelope and examining each and every name on each and every slip of paper. And out of these countless slips of paper, a committee of experts selected just one name and address whose owner was to receive a lavishly appropriate gift, absolutely free, no strings attached. Do you want to know whose name and address was on that slip of paper chosen from among countless other slips of paper by a committee of experts?

Of course I did want to know, says Parson Smith, who wouldn't? But at that moment, I could not respond to his question because shortly before that moment I had become seized with a nameless emotion. In fact, I was weeping hotly and hot tears were streaming in multiple rivulets down my face. My better half!! I sobbed. My better half from this not as good half has been torn asunder!!!

You were distressed, says Sherry, about the prolonged absence or possibly irrevocable loss of your better half, Mary Smith. Possibly, says Parson Smith. The cabby certainly took it for distress and he responded with more sympathy than I would have expected.

He got out of his cab, sat on the curb beside where I was sitting, pulled from his pocket a large pink and white checked hanky and applied it tenderly to my streaming cheeks.

Look buddy, he said. I can see you're a man of genuine sentiment, and though normally I deliver these prizes perfectly indifferent as to who the recipient is, in this case, I feel a profound solidarity with the committee which has chosen you and dearly hope that you will accept the prize; not only because that will complete the errand to which I have been assigned, but also because I genuinely believe that you and only you deserve it.

Gosh, I said, blinking away my tears. What is the prize? Get in the cab, said the cabby, and I'll show you.

I only wish, I said, getting up, that my better half, Mary Smith, were here to enjoy this moment with me. Contrary to popular opinion, the cabby said, little is irrevocable in this world. I would not be at all surprised if after a series of excruciating but, in the end, gratifying trials, you were not reunited with her. You think so? I said. Why not? said the cabby, who had stepped over to his cab and opened the door. Hop in!

I hopped in, says Parson Smith, my canniness completely dispelled by the cabby's sympathetic and forthright manner. I continued to be completely open with him, but now it was no longer a stratagem but a reflection of genuine feelings of kinship and fraternity.

Did you know, I said, that I've communicated in a mysterious fashion with the beasts of the field? Huh? said the cabby. Squirrels mostly, and pigeons, I said, but I've also communicated with rodents of the rat variety. Rats? said the cabby. But I've found squirrels to be considerably more congenial, I said.

Why just a few days ago, I said, I found myself sitting on a park bench engaged in desultory conversation not only with a certain guy I habitually encounter at the hooch depot but also with a squirrel that was squatting on its haunches under a nearby tree, chucking its tongue. The guy from the hooch depot was telling me about a certain commandant and a certain execution that he was sure was going to take place in the near future. I was humoring him because he's always struck me as a bit of a twit, but at the same time I was mysteriously communicating with the squirrel.

See this committee of experts has been studying the problem for some time now, said the guy from the hooch depot, and they have determined that it's actually true that there are far too many when really there should be only one, and as a result many are extra and those extras must be dispatched. Although you were never specifically mentioned, I have a strong intuition that matter concerns you closely.

Ahh, yes, it concerns me closely, right, I said, and as I was humoring him, I was also communicating mysteriously with the squirrel. I said, though "said" is not the right word for it at all: Ho there observing woodland creature! What think you? These words and gestures that I and this other party are presently performing on this green park bench glazed with rain must appear strange if not wholly inscrutable to an alien creature such as yourself. And the squirrel "said": You couldn't be more wrong. Your words and gestures are entirely legible and lucid to me. In fact, I've been told all about them in advance. By whom? I said. Ask your better half, Mary Smith, "said" the squirrel.

Hey! That Mary Smith really gets around! said the cabby. You've seen her? I said. No, said the cabby. But I've heard about her from my lord and master, the great Oxahatamatamongo. Oxahata—what? I said. I believe he has been revealed to you only in his lesser aspect, said the cabby, that is as the figure habitually referred to as "the guy from the hooch depot" Ah ha! I said.

I said "Ah ha!" because just then I remembered where I had seen the deformed "cabby" before and it was indeed at the hooch depot, in fact, in the company of the one I had believed to be "the guy from the hooch depot" and if I remember correctly, at that time, they had been discussing no one other than my very own better half "Mary Smith." That is

Mary Smith, says Parson Smith. That's quite a coincidence, says Sherry. Is it? says Parson Smith, raising an eyebrow. Is a coincidence what it is?

I grew canny once again, says Parson Smith. How long exactly, I probed, have you been working for the guy who I used to know as "the guy from the hooch depot"? About ten years, said the cabby. That's a long time, I said. Precisely, said the cabby. I chose that figure arbitrarily. In truth I really don't know how long I've worked for my lord and master the great Oxahatamatamongo. I only know it's been a long time.

I confess, I said, returning to my stratagem of complete frankness, that I too have lost track of time. Even though the days with my better half, Mary Smith, were homogeneously blissful, toward the end, each day began to seem longer than the one before it. In fact, the last day, during which I performed various and minute ministrations on her person, seemed to go on forever. Hell, for all I know, it might still be going on right now, I said, said Parson Smith.

My lord and master often pondered such matters, said the cabby, and then he pointed out the window. Hey, isn't that that acquaintance of yours, Jack?

And it was Jack, trudging along the sidewalk with what appeared to be an oversized fowl beside him.

He's got a fowl with him, I said, and who are all those ne'er-do-wells walking behind him in single file? Search me, said the cabby. The way they are strung out behind him, I said, each in his multicolored and motley vestment strongly suggests to me a parade of some sort or a sacred procession. Could be, said the cabby. I wonder where they're going. I said. I don't know, said the cabby, but I have a strong intuition that you'll find out. When will we get to my prize? I said. Here we are, said the cabby, and he pulled off the street into a very large and grassy lot far outside the city.

We both got out of the cab and stood together on a hummock. The lot was very large, at least as large as the huge lot behind the big building in which conventions are sometimes held. But whereas that lot is brown and broken, this lot was immensely green and smooth. Its greenness and smoothness was also suffused with a receding spill of red on one side because the sun was going down there, and a growing spill of milky white on the other side because there the moon was rising.

When the moon had finally ballooned up completely above the horizon, the cabby turned to me and said, Well whaddaya think?—in reference, I believe, to the moon or the field, or possibly something completely absent.

It is large, I said, playing it safe. Yes, he said. But what'll I do with it? I said. That's up to you, said the cabby. But what if I can't think of anything to do with it? I asked, for in truth, I hadn't the slightest clue what to do with either the moon or the field or the thing wholly absent to which he might possibly be referring.

Then you can take this, said the cabby and he handed me the card I have recently given you, and said, At a certain establishment that I am happy to take you to, that card is good for all the hooch you can drink. All right! I said, and we hopped back in to the cab, and he brought me here.

To think, says Parson Smith, just this morning—if it was the morning—I was utterly despondent what with the prolonged absence if not irrevocable loss of my better half and all, but now—Parson Smith drains off the hooch in his glass, and slams the glass down on the bar—things, for me at least, are looking up!

I'll bet, says the ne'er-do-well, lifting his bandage-swaddled head off the bar. And I mean that skeptically. It has been my experience that the sensation that "things are looking up" often functions as an indicator of precisely the opposite condition.

Oh Henry, says Sherry. Henry? says Parson Smith. Haven't I seen you someplace before, at a convention perhaps? The whistler! says Henry. Right, says Parson Smith. Wicker? Bingo! says Henry. But weren't you wearing ear-rings? says

Parson Smith.

Yes, says Henry, I was. But my ears have been mutilated by a recent female acquaintance of mine. I have applied bandages and plaster to speed the healing process and conceal their present unsightliness. Your ears are unsightly? says Parson Smith. Yes, they are, says Henry. I see, says Parson Smith. No, you don't says Henry. Their mutilation was an act charged with symbolic significance for the acquaintance who mutilated them. I see, says Parson Smith. No, you don't, says Henry. Even I remain ignorant of the nature of that symbolism. For me, the act was quite literal and aside from producing an intense and poignant itch behind my ears, meaningless. In fact, as far as I can tell, my hearing has been unaffected. That's lucky, says Parson Smith. You loved her, says Sherry. She left me with this, says Henry and he bends down and pulls a huge, furry purse from below his stool and slams it on the bar. Goodness! says Parson Smith. Oh my! says Sherry.

Just look inside, says Henry. Just take a look! And tell me if "things are looking up." Then you can tell me if Jack is "Jack" or a different "Jack". Or whether the guy from the hooch depot is "the guy from the hooch depot" or Oxahatamatamongo or "Oxahatamatamongo" or a different "Oxahatamatamongo"? Oxahata—what? says Parson Smith. Or maybe, says Henry, just maybe, you can tell me what time it is for God's sake. That seems like a simple, run of the mill, question doesn't it? Or is it too much to ask?

Relax, Henry, says Sherry who has been rifling through the purse. It's quarter after eleven. Sherry points absently to a clock above the bar with big, clear numbers. It reads quarter after eleven. Hey! says Sherry. There are two videos in here!

Great! says Parson Smith. I love videos even though when I watch them, I rarely have a clue as to what's going on. Me too! says Sherry. Henry, who has buried his head once again in his arms, makes a gurgling noise.

We should watch them now, says Sherry, as in addition to the usual fare here, there is to be a grand entertainment on the main stage in just a little while and I've heard from a reliable source that it's not to be missed. Y'hear that, Henry? says Parson Smith. A grand entertainment! On the main stage! Not to be missed! Hey guy! Cheer up!

Just watch the videos, says Henry, without raising his head.

Sherry has already inserted one of the videotapes into a box below the T.V. above the bar. The machine hums and whirrs. The screen on the T.V. remains blank for a moment, but then, in the manner of a great gray eye opening, it is filled with light.

Hey! That looks a lot like the hooch depot! says Parson Smith. Quiet! says Sherry. I want to hear what's going on.

The hooch depot is a box of white light. The guy from the hooch depot, the Great Oxahatamatamongo, as it turns out, is standing on the counter in the glare, gesturing grandly. Jack and his father crouch on the floor below.

The Great Oxahatamatamongo (declaiming): Yes gentlemen, I remember. I remember that night when the father of Jack's father, the grandfather of Jack, well along in the course of his diminution, crept under the crack of the door of my former more kingly bedroom and scaled the bedspread of my former and more kingly pallet, and ascended my shoulder in hops like a bed bug, and attained the cataract of my ear, and in the shelter of my magnanimous ear fold related to me the obscure rambling that he had stumbled across in his extensive wanderings to regions even more distant and obscure than the one I then inhabited.

Jack: More obscure and distant?

The Great Oxahatamatamongo: Considerably. Not only were these regions obscure and distant but also, in several cases, nameless, which makes it twice as hard to talk about them.

Jack: I see.

The Great Oxahatamatamongo: Shut up! Slave! The upshot of the obscure rambling related to me by your grandfather had a direct bearing on the actions of my royal personage and thus, through me, all those fortunate enough to pass within my sphere.

Jack: That's us.

The Great Oxahatamatamongo: Exactly. The upshot was this: though when circumstances demand it, my position allows me to transgress even the holiest of codes without so much as a shrug of the shoulder, there are certain completely arbitrary and some might say trivial prohibitions that even I am compelled to observe with unvarying regularity.

Jack: The hooch?

The Great Oxahatamatamongo: I'm sorry. I just can't sell hooch to a feathered but flightless biped of that size.

Jack: No hooch?

The Great Oxahatamatamongo: None here. But take this map and follow the directions printed thereon to a certain establishment. I have a strong intuition that there your request will be vouchsafed.

The screen goes blank.

Hmm..., says Parson Smith. Hmm..., says Sherry. Well, says Parson Smith, those guys looked really familiar to me but I can't quite place them.

Put the next one in, says Henry without lifting his head from the bar. Is it long? says Sherry, 'cuz the show's gonna start in a little while, and you'll want to get a table right up front.

I have a strong intuition, says Henry, rubbing first one side of his head and then the other against the bar, that it's just long enough.

Say..., says Parson Smith, but his attention is distracted by a small dark movement in a far corner of the establishment near the bathroom. The small dark movement is being performed by a rat, which, upon noticing the attention directed on it by Parson Smith, pauses in front of the crack in the bathroom door. That rat has a bare worm-like tail, yellow eyes and bits of white viscid material gathered where the seal of its black lips is broken by irregular and sharply pointed teeth. Parson Smith: Is existence a difficult and inconvenient undertaking for a vile creature such as yourself? Rat: Not in any way with which you might sympathize. Parson Smith: How do you know? Rat: Ask your better half, Mary

Smith. Parson Smith: You've been in touch with her? Rat: For some time now. Parson Smith: Over and out. Rat: So too, I go on.

The machine hums and whirrs. The screen is the blackest of black, but then the gray eye opens.

That place looks mighty familiar, says Sherry. Funny, it also appears familiar to me, says Parson Smith. Just watch, says Henry.

On the screen, Jack and his father are standing on the sidewalk under the awning in front of a certain establishment. Streetlights from somewhere off screen throw dirty puddles of yellow light around them. A sizable and murmuring crowd of ne'er-do-wells have gathered in the shadows. Jack appears to be talking to himself.

Jack: Considering that you don't have features with which I might identify you as I am conversing with you right now, I don't see why you would think it would be possible for me to match you with the memory I may or may not have of a person or entity with whom I have conversed in the past.

Jack's father (pecking disconsolately):

Jack: To be honest, I'm not altogether sure you exist. In fact, if it turned out that you didn't exist and I've been standing here under the awning of this certain establishment, talking to myself, I wouldn't be surprised at all. In fact, I think I would find that realization deeply confirming.

Jack's father (looking out at the crowd of ne'er-do-wells):

Jack: In fact, it strikes me as not at all unlikely that even I am not here.

Jack's father (pecking nervously at the concrete):

I swear I've seen that guy someplace before, says Parson Smith. Jack, says Henry, it's Jack. You think it's the same one? says Sherry. Erger er ger er ger, says Henry. I mean the same one that habitually comes in here wearing a disguise, says Sherry.

Say..., says Parson Smith, but his attention is again distracted by a dark movement in a far corner of the bar. This movement is also being performed by a rat. But this rat is a good deal larger than the first, and though its eyes are equally yellow they also give off white glints of fever. Parson Smith: Are you aware that a creature as vile as yourself though not as large has recently slipped through the door, which you are about to slip through? Rat: What of it? Parson Smith: Over and out. Rat: So to, I go on.

Jack: The hooch in there is terrible. Besides I think I've lost my taste for it.

Ne'er-do-well 1 (from the shadows): Hooch?

Jack's father (looking at Jack):

Jack: I don't want to go in there. I like it out here. It's kinda airy.

Ne'er-do-well 2 (from the shadows): Did he say "free hooch"?

Jack's father (looking with some degree of alarm at the crowd of ne'er-do-wells):

Jack: But what I like best is not so much being out here, assuming that that's where I am, but not being in there and all the other places where I'm not.

Ne'er-do-well 3: I remember the last time there was hooch available for whoever wanted it.

Jack: I like also the comforting sensation that nothing can really happen out here. Or rather, a lot of things could happen, but nothing that would make any difference.

Ne'er-do-well 4: If I remember correctly, I was an upright citizen before that event.

Jack's father (pecking gingerly and then more aggressively at the door to the establishment):

Jack: Who knows? If I wait here long enough, maybe Mona will show up.

Ne'er-do-well 5: After that, everything changed for me too.

Jack: It's equally possible that she won't show up.

Jack's father (sitting on the pavement):

Ne'er-do-well 6: It was in the course of that very special day that I realized that the consumption of hooch was` not so much an auxiliary activity attached to the mainstays of my existence but—

Jack: How would you know?

Ne'er-do-well 7: Rather more integral.

Jack: Quite frankly, I don't believe in "the guy from the hooch depot."

Ne'er-do-well 8: The significance with which I invested the repetitive work I had hitherto performed dwindled rapidly.

Jack: He looks like a twit and I wouldn't be surprised at all if all that "Oxahatamatamongo" business turned out to be an elaborate hoax.

Ne'er-do-well 9: I realized that the tinge of pleasure I had felt in performing that work stemmed not so much from the work itself but more from the currency I received for doing it.

Jack: Of course if it weren't a hoax...

Ne'er-do-well 10: And the more powerfully felt pleasure of receiving that currency stemmed not so much from the currency itself, but from the goods I received in exchange of it.

Jack: It wouldn't make any difference.

Ne'er-do-well 11: And one particular good counted for more than all the others.

Jack (sitting on the pavement beside his father):

Ne'er-do-well 12: One particular good embodied the essence of the pleasure, which was only contingent in all the others.

Jack:

Ne'er-do-wells 1 through 12 (emerging from the shadows): Hooch! Free hooch! Hooch on Jack!

The screen is filled with a confusion of bodies into which Jack and his father are swallowed up. For a moment Jack's ear can be spotted in the tumult of limbs and features, then his father's beak, then a cloudlet of feathers. Then the screen goes blank.

Boy, says Sherry, I sure wouldn't want to be either of those guys. It looks like the ne'er-do-wells are going to eat them alive.

Henry, who is rolling on the floor clutching the bloody pulp on the sides of his head with both hands, says nothing.

Say..., says Parson Smith, but he is once again distracted. The movements that he had observed by the bathroom door have been duplicated and reduplicated. A small caravan of large rats is disappearing in spurts through the crack. Parson Smith: Ho there fellow travelers! What moves you so repetitively in yonder region? Rats: It's none of your business. Parson Smith: Why not? Rats: Ask Mary Smith. Parson Smith: The whole lot of you? Rats: We're only the beginning. Parson Smith: Over and out. Rats: So too, we go on.

Do you think he's O.K.? says Parson Smith, in reference to Henry who has ceased rolling and now lays on the ground completely inert. He's fine, says Sherry. I don't know, says Parson Smith.

Henry! says Sherry to Henry, who in truth doesn't look much like Henry at all anymore but more like a vaguely human figure abbreviated at the top into a pulpy mass of blood. You'd better take your pal Parson Smith here to a table in front if you want to get a good seat for our special entertainment. The joint is filling up. Right, says Henry, through his wounds as he struggles to stand up.

Sherry: I had a rattan chair once, but what I really wanted was wicker. It was my ambition to obtain that wicker chair after having already fallen into or stumbled over a verandah with a house attached to it, if you know what I mean. It's funny. I've never given much thought to the house. In fact, the house itself does not concern me the least bit, aside from, perhaps, the knowledge that the procurer of the house, that is the agent through whose good offices I had acquired it, might be inside sleeping, or lying in a more debilitated condition, prostrate in the heat, for example. He would be prostrate in the heat because the house would be located in a hot, hot place, and it would be twice as hot inside the house where the procurer would remain as outside the house where I would remain, enjoying the cooler breezes such as they were. And as I sat comfortably amidst the exhausted quivering exhalations of August, I would lavish contemplations on more pertinent matters, namely: my mother and her hat. Contemplating these, I would shrink further and further towards the unlocatable center of the vast and vaulted space of my mind, throughout which my contemplations would mesh as yarn meshes and bend and ripple as banners of cloth bend and ripple when suspended in endlessly gentle waters. So small and lost would I become that the passage of time would grow imperceptible to me. But of course, time would pass. The hot white sky would flare to an unendurable brightness at the peak of the afternoon, then fade abruptly into evening's smoldering orange, and finally, flicker out altogether, painting all vistas in the deepest shades of black.

Well, that should do the trick, says Parson Smith, pasting a final bar napkin to the head of Henry who sits across from him at a small table in front of the main stage. When my better half, Mary Smith, had problems of a similar nature, I always found bar napkins to be just the thing.

Parson Smith waves to Sherry at the bar. She hurries to the table with two tall glasses of hooch. Anything else? says Sherry. Is there anything else? says Henry. No, says Sherry. Then why did you ask? says Henry. Y'know with all those napkins plastered to your head, says Sherry, you look like a mullah.

Not a mullah, says Jack, who has sauntered up to the table with his father. But more of a fakir. The former indicates merely the learned and the latter, a teacher.

Jack! says Parson Smith. Parson Smith! says Jack. Rattan! says Henry. He's Henry, says Parson Smith. This is my dad, says Jack. Jack's father says nothing. Jack takes a seat at the table.

Have you come to see the show? says Parson Smith. And get more hooch, says Jack. Say, where's your better half, Mary Smith? Where's the little guy who used to hang out in your apartment? says Parson Smith. I don't know, says Jack, and though at first, I admit, I felt everything but regret at his absence, now I kind of miss him. I too am a truncated being, says Parson Smith. I like to think, says Jack, even though I have virtually no evidence to suggest it, that the little guy continues to exist somewhere beyond my knowledge of him. Perhaps, says Parson Smith, you can take a measure of comfort in his very absence, which, in its dimensions and precise outlines, may evoke in the viscid and distorted sphere of your consciousness his very presence as a thumb print in a pat of butter evokes the absent thumb. Well put, says Jack. Thanks, says Parson Smith.

I wish you both would shut up, says Henry.

Hey! says Parson Smith. Aside from the mass of napkins swaddling Henry's head, you two look exactly alike.

What of it? say Jack and Henry at the same time.

Funny, says Parson Smith, I had this idea that you'd been devoured by a pack of ravenous ne'er-do-wells. No, I made a deal with them, says Jack. They're really a great bunch of guys once you get to know them. Really? says Henry.

Really, says Jack. But in need of instruction. In your present guise, I don't suppose you'd be willing to address them? Hmm...says Henry. You might do them some good, says Jack, and I'm sure you would find the experience rewarding as well.

You really think, says Henry, that in my present guise I create the impression of harboring secret knowledge? Sure, says Jack. I think I deserve it, says Henry. If I were you, says Jack, I wouldn't let that knowledge go to waste but go out there right now and share what you know with the ne'er-do-wells. You think they'd appreciate it? says Henry. Sure, says Jack. Why not? says Parson Smith.

Henry departs.

More hooch! says Jack. Here here! says Parson Smith. It's on me. Sherry brings them hooch wordlessly. That's great hooch! says Parson Smith, though I've heard it's adulterated.

Do you think, says Jack, if one, just suppose, if one heard voices, say in one's head, or at least in the close vicinity of one's head, one ought to, in the event that these voices began discoursing in the imperative mood, one ought to, in good conscience or out of a general pliability or perhaps because one has no other plans, obey them?

Parson Smith pauses with his glass at his lips. Jack's father pauses with his beak immersed in his glass. Henry pauses before the front door of the establishment.

Are you crazy? they all say at the same time.

The establishment is packed. Some of the ne'er-do-wells who had gathered outside have come in and multiplied and now occupy all the small and medium-sized tables in the joint as well as the barstools. Sherry has also multiplied. Several bony horse-faced girls circulate among the tables replenishing the hooch glasses of the ne'er-do-wells. The voices of Parson Smith, Jack's father and Henry, wound together in that single sentence, float like a braid of yarn and string above the general hubbub.

Henry slips out of the front door of the establishment.

It would be unwise and morally reprehensible to do so, says one of the Sherrys bringing a fresh glass of hooch and refilling the glasses already on the table. Whither comes this voice or these voices? From a place fair or foul? Have these voices the clarion ring of righteousness or the dry rasp of damnation? Can you, confused subject that you are, immersed in your own fetid particularity as a rotting log in a malarial swamp, claim the perspicacity to distinguish them? I think not.

I think not, say all the other Sherry's pausing in their tasks.

Agonized screams are heard from the street.

I think so, says a voice somewhere near Jack's shoulder. If you can't trust your grandfather, who can you trust?

Grandpa? says Jack. Dad? says Jack's father. I'm over here, says Jack's grandfather from a spot on the table. What's going on? says Parson Smith.

It's my grandfather, says Jack. We thought he had been infinitely diminished some time ago, but apparently we were wrong. Yes, says Mary Smith, who has emerged from the bathroom and glided to the table. If in truth he had started infinitely diminishing some time ago, he would still be infinitely diminishing right now, wouldn't he?

Mary Smith! says Parson Smith. Mary Smith! says Jack. Yeah? says Mary Smith.

You look different, says Parson Smith. That's because I'm dead, says Mary Smith. You and the doctor killed me. Uhh sorry, says Parson Smith. It's O.K., says Mary Smith. I kinda like it. I'm pals with the rats now, and they've invited me to be in their show. Bye!

Mary Smith glides up to the stage and passes through a narrow gap in the curtains, which part to receive her.

Son, you've become a feathered but flightless biped, says Jack's grandfather. What do you have to say for yourself? It wasn't my fault? says Jack's father through his beak. I can attest to that, says Jack. It had something to do with those two children and the rat.

That's a crock, says Mona, who has appeared beside the table from someplace else without passing through the intervening space. The little guy, bathed in light, sleeps in her arms. There never were any rats or any children. It's all been a lot of hooey!

Mo-Mo-Mo, says Jack.

Order me more hooch, baby, says Mona. And tell your forefathers to hurry up and get on stage. The show's gonna start any minute.

We're gone, say Jack's father and grandfather at the same time.

Say, says Parson Smith, but he is distracted by a wave of small dark movements flooding under the tables and up onto the apron of the main stage. Parson Smith: Is the show going to start soon? Rats: You better believe it! Parson Smith: Are you going to be part of the show? Rats: And you too, you better get up here. Parson Smith: Over and out. The rats: So too, we go on.

I've gotta go, says Parson Smith to Jack.

Baby, where have you been? says Jack to Mona. I saw a talking dog, says Mona. It was eating peanut butter? says Jack. No, that was the magnate, says Mona. And where did you find the little guy? says Jack. I don't remember, says Mona. It's great that he's sleeping, says Jack. Yeah, says Mona. He shut up sometime ago and hasn't opened his mouth since. Wow! says Jack. He might be practicing for the show, says Mona. That's his part. He plays the little guy who sleeps. I play a different part. I play the person who wings it. Who am I? says Jack. You just watch, says Mona, rising. That's your part. You play one of the guys who just watches.

Say Mona, says Jack. Are you sure you want to be in the show? Want to be? says Mona.

Why don't you stay here? says Jack, and play the person sitting next to one of the guys who just watches. I don't think so, says Mona. I don't like the looks of that curtain, says Jack. The way it has gulped down Mary Smith, Parson Smith, my father and my grandfather is disturbingly reminiscent of the way a very large insect might consume its prey; that is with long, vertical jaws.

Bye Jack, says Mona dematerializing along with the little guy.

Wait! says Jack. Isn't that the guy from the hooch depot!?

Jack points to the edge of the stage where a human figure is attempting to clamber up onto the apron.

Could be, says Mona, flickering briefly into existence, but the elaborate ceremonial garb he is wearing makes certain identification impossible. Bye!

That's my lord and master the great Oxahatamatamongo, says the cabby as he rushes past Jack's table. Glad you could make it, says Jack, sit down and have some hooch the show is sure to be...

But Jack desists mid sentence as the cabby vaults onto the apron and disappears behind the curtain.

The lights in the establishment go down and a general hush falls over the crowd of assembled spectators. Jack watches the still expanse of the vast curtain for some time. Finally, he detects a ripple of movement.

Here we go, says Jack, under his breath.

ABOUT THE AUTHOR

James Lewelling is also the author of *This Guy* (Spuyten Duyvil, 2005) and *Tortoise* (Calamari Press, 2008). He has been writing fiction since 1988 while at the same time teaching and working in Morocco, Turkey and the U.A.E. At present, he is living and writing in Abu Dhabi.

www.ingramcontent.com/pod-product-compliance
Lightning Source LLC
Chambersburg PA
CBHW060104260626
47160CB00005B/1789